LORI & MAX

Catherine O'Flynn

First published in 2019
by Firefly Press
25 Gabalfa Road, Llandaff North, Cardiff, CF14 2JJ
www.fireflypress.co.uk

A CIP catalogue record of this book is available
from the British Library.

ISBN 9781913102029

This book has been published with the support of
the Welsh Books Council.

Typeset by Elaine Sharples

Printed and bound in Great Britain by Clays Ltd, Elcograf S.p.A

For Edie and Dory

I'm not saying I have superpowers. I can't even run very fast (third slowest in class in fact), let alone see into the future, but somehow before I even get to school I can tell something bad is going to happen today. Maybe it's a kind of undercover detective instinct. Or maybe it's just that it feels like all this week has been building up to something big.

When I get to the classroom, I see I was right. A man and woman I don't recognise are standing behind Miss Casey. They look super-serious. Miss Casey looks even more pale and worried than normal; she clears her throat to speak. Something is very definitely wrong, I just don't know quite how wrong yet.

'Good morning, Class 6B. Please settle down and listen carefully. We have two police officers with us today: this is Detective Superintendent Alison Burrows and Detective Sergeant Steve Locke. I'd like you to pay very special attention to what they have to say.'

A buzz goes round the classroom – real life

detectives in school! Normally I'd be so excited I'd find it hard to stay in my seat, but the bad feeling I've had all morning tells me this isn't a fun visit.

'Good morning, children,' says serious-looking Alison Burrows. 'I'm sorry to have to tell you that one of your classmates, Maxine Ellington, has gone missing.' Everyone takes a sharp breath in at the same time but the detective carries on before anyone can speak. 'Maxine was last seen by her mum yesterday morning, when she went out on an errand. I want to make it clear that we have no reason to believe that Maxine has been taken by anybody. It's our belief that she has run away from home. We know she was in some trouble at school this week. We think she has a significant sum of cash and all evidence points to her heading off on her own. I'm sure you understand that we are concerned for her safety and well-being and I'm sure you will help us do everything we can to find her. We're going to be coming around and talking to each one of you this morning. If you have any specific information about Maxine's whereabouts of course we want to know but, failing that, anything at all that you might know about her could help us.'

I sit very still, staring straight ahead. There are things that only I know about Max. Things I've sworn never to tell.

'Lori? Lori Mason?'

I look up and see Detective Superintendent Alison Burrows standing at my desk.

'Miss Casey says that you're Max's closest friend.'

I nod.

'Then we have some questions we'd like you to answer. Can you come with me, please?'

Chapter One

Three months earlier

It's a typical Monday morning in Class 6B. Miss Casey is nowhere to be seen. Behaviour that she would definitely describe as 'unacceptable' is breaking out in every direction. Yasmin Oldershaw and Nina Masters are practising dance moves in the corner. Josh Ryman has tied Jessica Pemberton's plaits to the back of her chair. Harry Besley has already started on his packed lunch and Elijah Stephens is fast asleep.

I sneak my notebook from my pocket and write in tiny letters:

February 16
9.12 a.m.

Miss Casey – another of her Frequent Brief Disappearances. Where does she go during these unexplained absences?

Current FBD theories:

1   *The toilet? (Can anyone wee so much?)*
2   *Sneaky snacking in the staffroom?*
    (Does Casey have a family-sized tub of
    Celebrations or similar on the go?)
3   *Mr Wilson's office? (Are they in love??)*

I'm careful to keep the notebook out of sight of my classmates. The important thing when you're a secret detective is to detect secretly. This is because:

a) No one commits a crime in plain view; criminals get more careless when they think no one's watching. Detectives have to keep a low profile. Secret is best.

b) The children of New Heath Primary (my school) have been known to tease, poke fun, name-call and generally make life challenging for anyone who stands out from the crowd e.g. Estelle Hannah who played the violin, collected exotic spiders and left after just one term. It's generally best to avoid doing anything that might be considered 'freaky' or 'weird' e.g. observing other children covertly and recording details in a notebook. Secret is definitely best.

6

Out of the window I see Mr Cheetham making his way across the playground over to the bike sheds. Mr Cheetham is the school caretaker and is super-hard-working, especially, I've noticed, in the area of the bike sheds. I see him going in and out of them six or seven times a day, which is weird really as they never actually look that clean, but that just shows how devoted he is to fighting grime. Ha ha, he fights grime and I fight crime. It's a shame my top-secret status prevents me sharing this excellent joke with anyone else. I'm distracted from my playground surveillance by the sudden scraping of chairs and clatter of desks as everyone rushes back to their seats when they hear Miss Casey approach.

'Now, children,' she calls out. 'Settle down. Silence please. That's enough of... Oh!' It's only now Miss Casey realises that no one's making a sound. Class 6B is silent. We are all staring at the girl at her side – an extremely tall and skinny girl. Her clothes are noticeably too small, as if she's grown since getting dressed. On top of her head is the craziest, frizziest, wildest explosion of what I guess is hair, but I'm pretty sure I can see some kind of twig in there and there's definitely a feather sticking out above one ear. The best way to picture this girl is to imagine a spindly tree, with a wonky bird's nest on top.

'Right. Yes. That's more like it. Very good. Now, class, I'd like to introduce you to a new girl who'll be joining Class 6B from today. This is Maxine...'

'Max.' Tree-girl says in a bored-sounding voice.

'Sorry. Yes. You did say that already. This is Max ... that's short for Maxine, as I said ... Ellington.'

'Max-that's-short-for-Maxine-as-I-said-Ellington,' sniggers Simon Yarker. 'What a mouthful!' Miss Casey looks confused and Max-that's-short-for-Maxine stares straight ahead.

'Now, class, I want you to make ... Max, feel very welcome and I'd like a volunteer, please, to show Max how we do things here at New Heath Primary and be her special *buddy*.'

Miss Casey makes invisible speech marks in the air when she says 'buddy'. No one moves or makes a sound. It's the first time I've ever noticed just how loudly the tap in the corner of the room drips and how heavily Kelly Keogh breathes. Even

Cuddles, our psychopathic class hamster, is silent for once as if he, too, is desperate not to be noticed and picked for the job.

'Anybody? Anybody?' says Miss Casey. 'Come on now, 6B. This isn't very nice for Maxine, is it? Not really making her feel welcome. Leaving her standing here, on her own, while I literally *beg* one of you to just give her a helping hand.' She turns briefly to Tree-girl. 'I'm sure it's nothing personal. Well, you know, not really...'

Tree-girl sighs like a grown-up; she rolls her eyes like a teenager; and then she walks past Miss Casey, makes her way straight across the room, and plonks her bag and herself down in the only available free seat, which happens to be right next to me.

Chapter Two

It's just another new school for Max; another new classroom; another new neighbourhood; another new teacher. She's done it so many times, nothing about it feels new at all. The teacher is the standard type: stressed, well-meaning. She's left the shop tag on her jumper – Max notices the plastic poking out of the back. Max prefers scatty teachers, the ones who leave price tags on clothes, the ones who forget. It's the ones who remember that she has to watch.

This one's a blue jumper school. The last one was red. The one before that was blue but a different blue. It doesn't make much difference. Max can usually get away without wearing the jumper or the tie. A grey skirt and a white polo shirt get her by. Mainly white anyway. There's a ketchup stain the shape of a tiny whale on the sleeve. She's tried scrubbing it with some shampoo but it won't come out.

The last school had loads of portacabins. The classrooms were baking hot in the summer and

10

freezing cold in the winter. Sometimes on icy days Max would keep her pyjama top on, hidden under her shirt. She thought it was better to do that than wear a jumper that was the wrong colour. A teacher would have noticed that. Max knows that if you keep turning up in non-uniform teachers start to wonder if there's a problem at home. They try to be kind and offer you stuff from lost property. If you take it, then they know there's a problem. Max tries to remember all the traps.

'It's a fresh start. We're leaving the past behind.' That's what her dad said when he walked her to school that morning.

'It's going to be different this time. I promise. I've got a good feeling about this place. We'll get settled, you just work hard and be a good girl and you'll make some nice friends.'

They reached the school gates. Max had a hollow, wobbly feeling inside. She noticed her dad had stopped walking. 'I won't come in, love. I've got some errands to run for your mum. You'll be alright by yourself, they know you're coming. Just remember: our luck's changing, Maxie.' He gave her a gentle push. As he walked away he tripped on a paving stone. He turned back to see if Max had seen.

In truth Max prefers animals to people. She thinks they're better in all kinds of ways. For one thing they're smarter. Animals are born with instinct, but people only learn by making mistakes. Max has changed school so often she has developed her own kind of instinct. If you've only ever been to one school, it might take you an entire term to get a sense of what everyone in your class is like. But if you change schools all the time, you get faster and better. Max absorbs information like a sponge now. She isn't even really aware she's doing it. She picks up on clues: familiar facial expressions, body language, clothes. Within ten minutes of walking into a classroom, she knows who are the bullies and who are the victims, who are the leaders and who are the followers. Her first impressions are almost always right. She can't afford to get them wrong. She's learnt that from animals: you've got to know who your predators are and never lose sight of them.

She can smell the irresistible waft of school-canteen pizza. Some days school dinner is the only meal she has. Her stomach rumbles but it's another three hours till lunch. She tries not to think about food. She wraps her fingers around the small silver snake charm in her pocket. She blocks out the classroom around her and imagines she's in the African savannah, sitting with a pride of lions basking in the sun.

Chapter Three

'Do you need a pencil?'

No response.

Maybe she hasn't heard me. I try again, whispering a little more loudly.

'Excuse me, erm … Max? … I've got a spare pencil if you want to borrow it.' In fact, I have sixteen pencils, twenty-two gel pens, a pineapple-scented rubber and a pencil sharpener that looks like an old-fashioned telephone box, but I don't want to overload her with information. 'Keep it relevant' is one of my mottos.

Tree-girl turns her head sharply. 'Hmm?'

'You don't seem to have a pencil and you need one to do the worksheet. You can borrow one of mine if you like.'

Tree-girl looks at me as if I'm speaking a foreign language. I speak more slowly. 'It's just, you haven't written anything yet. We have to hand them in before playtime,' I look at my watch (digital, thirty-six functions; again, I don't overload her with the details), 'which is in five minutes' time. You might get into trouble.'

I'm not a fan of trouble. Even for other people. Even people I don't know. Even people with really extraordinarily crazy hair. Maybe that's why I'm a detective. I want to nip trouble in the bud, stop trouble in its tracks, prevent trouble from getting out of bed...you get the idea. But now Tariq, who sits opposite, looks up. 'She's probably got a pencil in her hair. Looks like she keeps everything in there – twigs, pencils, sandwiches, birds probably.'

I try to stop worrying that Max isn't doing what she's supposed to be doing and turn my attention instead to the 'Christine Aisley Dream Come True' collection box on the wall. I try and count all the money inside. It's actually completely impossible to do, but it's an excellent way to distract yourself when the person next to you is behaving in a way that is making you feel a little bit anxious. Christine Aisley is the older sister of Kieron in my class. Christine has leukaemia and so we're raising money to send her to the Great Wall of China. Unbelievably, her lifelong dream is to see and possibly walk on what is essentially an excessively long, grey wall. Kieron says that if he was seriously ill, he'd think of way better things to do with people's charity donations. But it takes all sorts, that's what my nan says, anyway.

The collection box is made of thick see-through plastic, which lets us keep track of the progress we're making. I count £280 in there, but there are loads more notes hidden behind the ones I can see and I haven't even bothered with the big pile of coins at the bottom. I narrow my eyes and examine the padlock, making sure it hasn't been tampered with. 'Where money lives, crime lurks.' That's another one of my mottos. It sounds good when I'm talking to clients. Or at least I'm pretty sure it would do if I had any clients. It's important to sound professional when talking to potential customers. You need to use the right lingo. I've written a guide in my secret notebook on how to become fluent in cop-talk in four easy steps:

1) Find one of those TV channels that show back-to-back cop programmes all day long.

2) Sit down, equip yourself with remote control, pad, pen, family-sized bag of Maltesers and your own choice of soft drink.

3) Watch at least three to four hours of thrilling detective action.

4) Repeat every day for the entire school holidays,

And that's all there is to it. If the grown-ups you live with are the kind that don't like you watching four hours of television every day, then you might have to try reading some detective books instead. Reading a book takes longer and is slightly trickier to combine with Maltesers and soft-drink consumption but, on the bright side, you don't have to sit through commercials for opticians and slimming milkshakes every seven minutes.

I can't help noticing that the new girl still hasn't written anything on her worksheet. I decide to put one of my sixteen pencils on her desk so she has at least a chance of finishing on time, or even starting. Even just writing her name at the top.

Now Josh Ryman leans over.

'So … Max, what were you expelled for?'

Again, Max doesn't seem to hear, she just carries on looking out of the window.

'Hey you … Max … I'm talking to you…'

Suddenly she speaks and very loudly. 'Who says I was expelled?'

Miss Casey gives out a general. 'Silence, everybody, please!'

Tariq continues in a low voice, 'Yeah, but … were you?'

''Course she was,' says Josh.

I don't like Josh Ryman, but he's probably right. In the last two years, five new children have joined the class, and all of them had been excluded from one school or another. My nan says it's a vicious circle. The first time she said it, I thought 'Vicious Circle' was the name of a gang or something, made up of the kind of kids that stole other kids' sweets and pulled cats' tails, but I was wrong. Nan says 'vicious circle' is an expression meaning a bad situation that gets worse and worse. She says it is like a scab that you keep picking, making it bleed again and again, so it never heals. Nobody really wants to come to New Heath Primary any more because nobody thinks it's a very good school. So we have loads of spare room, which means there's always space for the kids other schools don't want. And the idea that our school is basically an enormous bin for unwanted children makes people even less keen on coming here, which makes more space for more unwanted children and so it goes on, round and round, like a circle. Not vicious really as far as I can see. If I had to use an adjective (or 'wow word' as Miss Casey insists on calling them), I'd say the circle was really more boring or annoying than vicious.

Miss Casey's calling out, 'Two more minutes, class. You should all be finishing off now. Please make sure that you've put your names at the top of your worksheets.'

Max's sheet is still blank.

'So, what were you expelled for?' Josh says again.

Max ignores him but finally picks up the pencil and starts doing some work.

'Oi, scarecrow!' says Tariq. 'Don't ignore Josh. Don't you know that's rude?'

Suddenly Miss Casey is at the table. 'Well, with all this chit-chat, I assume everyone here has finished their work and is ready to hand it in.'

Miss Casey always says 'chit-chat'. It's like nobody's told her that you don't need the 'chit' bit. Is chit even the same as chat? Nobody explains these things, least of all Miss Casey.

We slide our worksheets across the desk to her. All except one.

'And Maxine? How did you get on with the task?'

'One minute,' says Max, holding up her finger like she's the teacher. Miss Casey stands and waits, looking a bit awkward until Max finally puts her pencil down and pushes the piece of paper across the table. She looks directly at Josh and Tariq for the first time:

'You want to know what I was expelled for?'

Suddenly Miss Casey gasps. 'What on earth is this?' She slams Max's worksheet back on the table. There, covering the entire piece of paper is an amazing picture of Josh and Tariq: one of the best drawings I've ever seen. Their eyes, noses and mouths are perfect, but their bodies aren't like their bodies at all. Their bodies are something else entirely: something grey and furry, with dirty-looking claws.

Max, still ignoring Miss Casey, gives Tariq and Josh a big grin and says, 'If you really want to know, I got expelled from my last school and the one before that because I've got this bad habit of turning silly boys who bother me into rats.'

Chapter Four

Max lies on her bed looking at the *Wildlife Atlas of the World*. Between its hard covers Max can travel to the Appalachian mountains of North America, or the Great Lakes of East Africa, or the frozen waters of Antarctica. Books are the kinds of things that get left behind when her family has to move, but not this one. She makes sure this one always comes with her. She reads it every day and never gets bored. Even her mum has noticed.

'What you want to read about them wolves all the time for? Nasty things,' she says.

'It's not just wolves, Mum,' says Max. 'It's every type of animal in the entire world. And anyway wolves aren't nasty. They only take what they need to survive.'

'You never met a wolf,' her mum says. As if she has. Max is fairly sure that the wildest animal her mum has ever seen is a cow. And even that made her scream.

Max would be completely happy to lie on her

bed all day long and lose herself in her book but the problem is that it's hard to concentrate, hard to travel through time and space and race through a meadow with a snowshoe hare, when the smell of fried food is driving her completely mad.

Max lives above a fried-chicken takeaway called Rooster Party. The name really bothers her. It's obviously not a party for the roosters. The thought of a big queue of happy chickens thinking they're going off to a party when in fact they're headed for a deep-fat fryer makes Max really sad. It also makes her feel bad that she likes eating chicken so much. When she comes home from school, she always stops and stares at the photos in the window of Rooster Party. There are chicken wings, chicken breasts, chicken nuggets, chicken kebabs, chicken that's been pulled and something called chicken popcorn. Max has no idea what that is. Popcorn for chickens? Popcorn made out of chickens? Whatever the type of chicken, it's always photographed in a box with chips and a can of Coke on the side. Max thinks this must be because Rez, who owns Rooster Party, has to spend so long coming up with crazy things to do with chickens that he's got no imagination left for anything else. The chicken looks very orange in all the photos and the chips looks pale and sweaty. But, even though the photos give her a headache, the name makes her sad and the smell isn't great, the constant waft from Rooster Party makes Max hungry all the time.

She heads out of her bedroom and across to the kitchen to scout around for food. All she manages to find are some teabags and the last handful of slightly stale Rice Pops. Her mum is asleep on the sofa. Max gently shakes her shoulder.

'Oh!' Her mum smiles. She always smiles when she wakes up, surprised and a little embarrassed that she has fallen asleep again. 'Did I nod off?'

'Mum, I'm hungry.'

'Did you want me to make you something?'

'There's nothing to make. We need to go shopping.'

'Well, where's your dad? He said he was going to the shop this morning.'

This is how it always starts. Max says nothing.

Her mum sits up. 'Get my purse. You go, will you, baby? I'm tired. Get something nice for yourself. I'll cook it for you when you come back.'

Her mum calls to her as Max hunts for the handbag in the hall. 'Should be a £20 note in there. I got it yesterday. Take it and buy whatever we need.'

Max finds the bag, opens the purse.

'You got it?' Her mum calls.

The purse is empty. He's taken it. She can't face telling her mum.

'I've got it,' she calls. 'Be back in half an hour.' She looks in at her mum before leaving. She's settling back down to sleep. Max wonders if she's eaten anything at all today. She grabs her jacket and feels for the snake charm in her pocket. Time to go hunting.

Chapter Five

'Got you a little present, sweetheart,' says Nan after we've finished tea, holding up a Ritzy carrier bag. Ritzy is a shop on New Heath high street. It sells clothes, usually with lots of glitter or pictures of fluffy animals on them. I find everything in Ritzy either confusing or crazy, but Nan loves it.

'You didn't have to get me a present, Nan.'

'Don't be daft. It was only cheap. Come on, try it on.'

That's the other problem with Ritzy. It's super-cheap. If there are two things in this world that my nan can't resist, they are bargains and clothes that make you look slightly crazy. Nan herself is a big fan of hats. She has hundreds of them. Some of them are OK, and by OK I don't mean something that I would ever wear, but OK meaning something an older lady might wear, on a very cold day when a hat is absolutely necessary. But most of them are not so OK (e.g. her 'hot pink pom-pom number') and she wears them whatever the weather.

I should say that Nan is not mad; overall she's an excellent nan. My mum and dad died when I was four months old and Nan came to live with me. She brought her clothes, her photos, her ceramic angels and her hats, but apart from that she left the house exactly as it was and I'm glad about that. I like knowing that this is where my parents lived and I love our house. It's old but not creepy old. It's almost always sunny and warm. The only thing is that sometimes it feels a bit like we're living in a museum where none of the exhibits have labels. Everything in the house is a bit of a mystery to us: the books, the ornaments, even the strange kitchen utensils. We look at the pictures hanging on the walls and wonder what they are. So Nan and I come up with our own names for them: like the sad-looking man on the landing is called 'Sourpuss' and the painting of the woman with eyes in the wrong place is called 'Wonky Chops'. Sometimes we come across one of the pictures somewhere else and find out its real name, or who painted it, or what it's supposed to be. Back in Year 2 we studied an artist called Henri Matisse and that's how I discovered that the massive picture in the living room that Nan and I both love was painted by him and is actually called 'The Snail'. I like Matisse, but he was obviously rubbish at titles. It looks nothing like a snail, so we stick with 'Woman with shopping bags', which is what it looks like and is anyway just a better thing to paint a picture of. Nan and I see eye to eye on most things. Unfortunately clothing is not one of them.

Nan pulls a purple T-shirt out of the Ritzy bag. It has jewels, possibly not real ones, all around the neck and on the front is a big picture of a puppy wearing glasses with the words 'Follow Your Dreams' written underneath.

'What do you think?'

I stare at it for a while trying to work it out. Is the puppy telling me to follow my dreams? Or is the T-shirt telling the puppy to follow his dreams? Do puppies have dreams? I'm fairly sure they don't wear glasses.

'He's cute, isn't he?' says Nan.

'What does it mean?'

Nan frowns and turns the T-shirt round to look at it. 'Mean? I don't know, love. I didn't read it. Nobody reads the words on clothes. It's fashion! You just go with it!'

'Right, I see.'

'You will wear it, won't you?'

'Yes, I'm sure I will.'

Nan gives me the look she gives when she thinks I'm fibbing. An eyes-narrowed, interrogating-detective-sergeant kind of look. 'Are you being polite?'

'I'm always polite. It's good to be polite.'

'It's not good to fib!'

'I will wear it, honestly.'

Nan shakes her head. 'Oh, I know, underneath one of your hoodies where no one can see it. People will think it's my doing. They'll look at you and think, "Poor love – lives with her nan – no idea what young girls should wear."'

'No one notices what I wear, Nan.'

'I don't want you to look different from the other girls. They all have their mums buying them the latest fashions. I don't want you looking the odd one out. The fuddy duddy.'

'The whatty whatty?'

'Fuddy duddy. You know – old fashioned, out of touch.'

'Nan, I'm not sure anyone says that any more.'

'Are you telling me that saying "fuddy duddy" is fuddy duddy?'

This makes me smile. 'Nan, the thing is, detectives don't have time to follow fashion or spend valuable minutes working out what puppies are thinking. We have our minds on other things. Plus, I'm meant to be undercover! Sherlock Holmes didn't have sequins on his deerstalker, did he?'

'Oh, the detective thing again. Lovey, you're ten years old. You're a child!'

This makes me actually splutter. 'Nan, there have been literally loads of child detectives!'

'Yes, love, in books. On telly. Not in real life.'

'Well, grown-up detectives have to start somewhere. I'm learning the tricks of the trade. Anyway, I'm good at solving mysteries. You told me that.'

'Well, you are smashing at finding my glasses, I have to say.'

'There you go then.'

I help Nan clear up and then head upstairs to do my homework. My bedroom has yellow walls covered with hand-painted rainbows, stars, clouds, unicorns and all kinds of fairytale things. My mum and dad did them all when Mum was pregnant with me. Nan said they only meant to do one rainbow but they got a bit carried away. I like my room, I really do, but sometimes I wish it was just a little bit more … professional looking, the kind of room a detective might have. One of my favourite things to do is to sit at my desk (also yellow with a large rainbow covering the top) and imagine my perfect room. I imagine a whole bank of filing cabinets for keeping all my important case files and also for slamming angrily and making a really good *thunk* sound when things get tough or I've only got 24 hours to complete an investigation. I also want a big, grown-up desk, for doing all my paperwork, ideally with one of those springy, bendy lights that you can move up and down. Behind the desk I'll have an enormous whiteboard or high-tech pinboard of some sort, where I can stick pictures of suspects and victims and clues and draw lines and question marks between them. Maybe I'll even get the internet up on it, just in case I need to Google something. Most important, though, will be the chair. I'll have a big, leather, swivel chair, that not only goes round and round but also up and down when you pull a lever, and makes a nice hissing sound, like the ones in Paperclips Office Supplies.

I open my yellow rainbow desk to check my case files. It doesn't take long as I only have four of them.

Case one: Disappearance/possible theft
Client: Pam Southwell (aka Nan)
Details: Missing pair of bifocal glasses reported by client on June 26th.
Investigation: After questioning and close search of client's sitting room, glasses found down side of the sofa.
Result: Case closed

Case two: Disappearance/possible theft
Client: Pam Southwell (aka Nan)
Details: Missing pair of bifocal glasses reported by client on June 30th.
Investigation: After questioning and close search of client's sitting room, glasses found down side of the sofa.
Result: Case closed

Case three: Disappearance/possible theft
Client: Pam Southwell (aka Nan)
Details: Missing pair of bifocal glasses reported by client on August 1st.

Investigation: Advised client to check side of sofa. Glasses found. Further advised client to put glasses on chain to be worn around neck.
Result: Case closed

<u>Case four: Missing person (cat)</u>
Client: Pam Southwell (aka Nan) on behalf of Mrs Cromarty (at no. 52)
Details: Cat answering to name of Mr Socks (description: black with white paws, likes eating pork scratchings) last seen August 28th in front garden.
Investigation: After questioning and close search of street/garden, no trace of Mr Socks.

Current lines of enquiry:
- *Mr Socks has been taken by catnappers*
- *Mr Socks has gone to live with someone else who can offer a healthier diet*
- *Mr Socks did not look when crossing the road*
- *Result: Unsolved*

And that's it. I suppose I could have had more if I accepted other cases from Nan, but I've had to tell her that looking for glasses, purses, hats and slippers doesn't really count as detective work. I mean, I'm happy to help her look for the countless things she mislays every single day, but I can't be launching formal investigations every time, I've told her. 'It's a lot of paperwork, Nan. It's not really necessary.'

If only I'd solved the Mr Socks case. Unofficially, I have a pretty good idea what happened to him: I saw a squashed, black, furry shape at the edge of Nicholson Street a week after the disappearance. I couldn't be one hundred per cent sure it was Mr Socks and I couldn't face telling Mrs Cromarty anyway, so I kept the information to myself. But if I'd found Mr Socks alive and returned him home, word would have got around, maybe other neighbours might have come with their own mysteries to investigate. The cases would have started flooding in.

You see, the hardest part of being a detective isn't solving mysteries, it's finding mysteries to solve.

Chapter Six

She knows the sound now. A kind of shuffling, swishing noise mixed in with some thuds and grunts and the occasional swear word. This is the sound of Max's dad trying to move a large screen TV either up or down stairs. Max has heard it a lot. Up is generally good news, but down is always bad.

He used to always have a big grin on his face as he wrestled a giant flat-screen through the door. 'Look what I got you both! Come see, look! Sixty-five-inch screen, man!' And then the three of them would sit in front of the screen, taking turns with the remote, pressing the buttons like he told them. Her dad would be so proud, like he'd made the TV himself.

But it never lasted long. 'I'm gonna get you a better one, I swear. Top of the range, babe,' he'd lie to Max's mum just a few weeks later as he tugged the cables out the back and took it away again to sell.

Now he says nothing. TVs come and TVs go and nobody mentions it. Even Max's dad gets sick of pretending sometimes. It's the same with laptops, mobile phones, her mum's jewellery. Sometimes they're there; sometimes they're not.

Max gave up on the telly a long time ago. She's happy enough with her book. Her mum likes looking at it, though, right up until he takes it away. On a good day, her head jerks and she frowns and says, 'Hey! What you doing? I was watching that.' On a bad day, she doesn't really react. She just carries on staring at the place where the telly was. Like the blank wall is the next programme.

The telly's still there at the moment. So things aren't at rock bottom. But Max's dad hasn't been home in four days and that can only mean one thing. He's gambling again.

Chapter Seven

Miss Casey is late again for registration and most of the class are 'horsing around', though if I were a horse, I'd be quite cheesed off about that particular expression. I mean, horses don't really 'horse around', they're generally quite sensible and well-behaved – boring even. I have never, for example, seen a horse steal someone's pencil case and start throwing it to his mates, as Josh Ryman has just done while Jessica Pemberton runs around frantically trying to get it back.

On the rare occasions when Josh Ryman isn't picking on someone, he's going on about his new trainers, or his bike, or the latest X-box games he's been bought. He tells everyone how much everything costs – he's like a walking, talking Argos catalogue. He's the first boy in the class to have a phone and, of course, it's the latest iPhone and he thinks it's totally unfair that he's not allowed to bring it into school. He's always been the biggest in the class – even back in Reception.

In fact, apart from expanding, he hasn't changed that much in either appearance or behaviour since he was four. He still has the same babyish face – slightly chubby, red cheeks and big blue eyes topped off with a floppy mop of blond, curly hair. Nan once said that he looked like an angel, which made me snort so much that some chocolate milkshake came out of my nose. I said: 'Nan, appearances can be very deceptive.'

'Children. Really. Settle down. Children. Really.' Miss Casey marches in late, clapping her hands. The only way to know Miss Casey is clapping is to actually see her do it, as she has this unfortunate disability where her claps make absolutely no noise. I'm not sure if she has extra-padded palms (she's generally quite skinny, but maybe all the fat is stored in her hands: is that possible?) but I consider her silent clapping quite a phenomenon of nature. I slip my secret notebook out and add to the list:

Current theories re Miss Casey's FBDs
4   Taking time out to practise clapping?

I sometimes wonder if Miss Casey is cut out for teaching. There are some skills that are essential for being a teacher. 'Must haves' is what they call them in the job adverts in the paper, but in Miss Casey's case (Casey's case – ha ha!) they'd have to call them 'haven't gots'. As well as clapping, Miss Casey finds it pretty much impossible to remember names, which is probably important for a teacher. Some days she's better than others, but on the bad days she's really bad. She calls Aleesha, Anita; Stacey, Kelly; Lauren, Jessica; and every boy is Colin, which is a whole other mystery as there isn't a single Colin in the school!

Current theories re. Miss Casey's FBDs
5   *Could Colin be the key? Who is Colin??*

But skills aren't everything. I like Miss Casey and I think overall, even with the 'haven't gots', she's a good teacher. She once spent the whole day teaching on roller-blades (despite the fact that she can't skate and fell over seventeen times) just to raise money for the Christine Aisley fund.

'Settle down, please, Class 6B!' she says now, finally giving up on the silent clapping. 'Today we're going to be doing something really quite exciting.' This is another issue Miss Casey has. She always misuses the word 'exciting'. She only ever uses it to describe things that are in fact the exact opposite of exciting. 'Today we're going to be learning a new method of long division. And here's the fun part – it's called the Bus Stop Method!' This is what I'm talking about: sky-diving equals exciting; crime fighting equals exciting; long division equals Miss Casey's idea of exciting.

'So, who can remind us: what is the opposite of division? Come on now, class.' She smiles. 'This is a question for babies. I expect to see everyone with their hands up.' A few more raise their arms. 'Good, better. Now, who's still hiding? Aha...' I know what's coming next. '...Maxine. I don't see your hand.'

Max never puts her hand up. After much up-close surveillance I've concluded that Max doesn't do any of the things that pretty much everyone else in the class does. She doesn't fidget in her seat, she doesn't chat during lessons; she doesn't repeat funny lines from films or practise street dance in the playground or whisper secrets to other girls. Max is definitely a bit odd.

The only thing is, I can't help noticing that I don't do too many of those things either, which makes me wonder: am I as weird as Max? I just seem to like different things from everyone else. Take Paperclips Office Supplies for example, which is in my opinion the best shop in the world. But no one else seems to think so. The girls in 6B are always going on instead about Snazzle which basically sells an unbelievable number of things to put in your hair and on your nails. I went there once (Nan made me) and tried some of their nail varnish (ditto) but it wouldn't dry and everything I touched got stuck to my nails – bits of pencil sharpenings, biscuit crumbs, small flying insects. It was like having ten small, self-adhesive litter traps attached to the ends of my fingers. That's Snazzle for you – I just can't see the appeal. Paperclips on the other hand is a ginormous warehouse full of absolutely essential items: rubber bands, ink pads, whiteboards, gel pens, every kind of pencil imaginable. The Paperclips catalogue is one of my very favourite things to read. Is that weird?

One of the reasons Nan's not so keen on my detective work is that she thinks I should 'mix more'. They are the exact words she always uses. She thinks if I 'mix more' I'll make more friends or even just one friend. I'm not really sure about that. What exactly is this mixing anyway and how do I do it? Do I just start circling random people in the playground, calling out: 'Hey, I'm Lori. Let's mix more!' Personally, I think that could fall into the 'quite odd' category.

But even if I don't have loads in common with the rest of the class, it doesn't mean I like the idea of having anything in common with Max. The truth is that I find it pretty stressful sitting next to her. It isn't that she does anything bad, it's more that she doesn't do anything at all: no maths, no spelling and grammar, no comprehension, not even any art, which she's obviously brilliant at. She just sits very still, like one of Nan's ceramic angels, looking straight ahead as if Miss Casey, the classroom and everyone in it is like the boring telly they always have on in the doctor's waiting room with the sound turned down.

Miss Casey has now finished explaining the Bus Stop method of long division. It hasn't worked for me at all. In fact I'd probably know more about long division right now if I'd spent the morning actually sitting at a bus stop rather than listening to Miss Casey. I'm staring at the long sloping lines of numbers on the whiteboard when Miss Casey calls out, 'Lisa?' I wait a moment and then raise my hand.

'Do you mean me, miss?' Miss Casey often calls me Lisa.

'Yes, of course I do. Could you come up for a quiet word, please?'

Alarm bells start ringing. I don't like the sound of 'a quiet word'. 'A quiet word' is well-known teacher code for a super-serious telling-off. Josh Ryman often has to go for a quiet word, sometimes with Mr Wilson, the head teacher. Aleesha Varley is always being sent for a quiet word with the lunchtime supervisor because of what she does with mashed potato. Once, an actual police officer turned up at school to have a quiet word with Archie Bell and he was never seen again! I've never been asked to have a quiet word with anyone. Even Max the ceramic angel seems to register something's up and turns to look as I get up from the desk and walk slowly to Miss Casey.

'So, Lisa…'

'Miss, I'm Lori, remember?'

'Lori!' She shouts as if she hasn't seen me for years. 'Of course you are! Sorry, Lori!' Then she laughs at that. It's not great having a name that rhymes with 'sorry'. People always start laughing when they apologise to me. 'Anyway, Lori, listen. I want to ask you a favour.'

'A favour?'

'Yes, a favour. I actually wanted to talk to you about Maxine Ellington.'

It's typical that the one name Miss Casey always remembers is Maxine's, when Maxine is the one person in the class who doesn't want to be called by their full name.

'I've noticed how well you and Maxine get along. Goodness me! Thick as thieves. Peas in a pod. You're getting on famously, aren't you?'

'Peas? Pod? Max? And me?'

'Yes. You pair of … big buddies.' (She makes those weird speech marks in the air again.)

'Buddies?'

'Chit-chatting away all day long.'

'Miss Casey, Max hasn't spoken a single word to me since she joined the class.'

'Well, OK, not chit-chatting. She's a quiet girl. But you rub along well together.'

'I don't know, Miss. We don't know each other at all.'

'The thing is, Lori, you are a very hard-working girl and Maxine ... well, she's still finding her feet here.'

I'm not sure Max is really looking that hard for her feet but I say nothing.

'I wondered if you'd be interested in a job?'

I like the idea of a job, ideally one that involves detective work but, failing that, any special role would be quite nice.

'What, like being a monitor?'

'Sort of.'

'It's not Hamster Monitor, is it? I don't think I could look after Cuddles; I don't think he likes me.'

'I'm not sure Cuddles likes any of us, Lori, with the possible exception of Josh, which is why he's Hamster Monitor. No, the role I was thinking of was that of ... Learning Mentor.'

'What is a Learning Mentor?'

'Well, it would be your job to help other children learn as well as you do.'

'Other children?'

'Well, just Maxine, in fact.'

'But I don't know how to do that, Miss.'

'Of course you do! If you just show her how you do things and encourage her to do the same, I think it would really help her.'

'But…' I realise I have no idea how to politely say, 'That's a terrible idea.' I trail off.

Miss Casey smiles. 'You're a superstar, Lori. I knew you'd have a go.'

I walk slowly back to my seat. I don't like the idea of telling Max what to do or how to do it. I'm not really someone who enjoys telling other people what to do and I have a pretty good idea that Max isn't the sort of person who enjoys being told either. I sit down, a bit lost in thought, and then I feel someone tapping my elbow.

'Let me guess what she just said.' These are the first words Max Ellington ever speaks to me.

'Go ahead.'

'She told you that you had to be my little helper, didn't she?'

I nod slowly and Max grins. 'Oh man – they always do that.'

Chapter Eight

Max is having her favourite dream. She has it quite often. She's inside an enormous sweet factory and her job is product tester. She sits by the side of an orange conveyor belt and helps herself to the endless variety of sweets and chocolates that glide past her. A man with a notebook stands beside her, carefully writing down her every pronouncement.

'More caramel needed.'

'Less crunch.'

'Good.'

'Good.'

'Outstanding.'

'Not sweet enough.'

She's reaching for a sour cherry bonbon when the man starts tapping her on the shoulder trying to tell her something. He starts shaking her gently and that's when she realises she's not dreaming any more. She wakes up to find her dad standing at the side of her bed. 'Happy birthday, sweetheart.'

It's still dark. She takes a minute to absorb the words and then she sits up, confused. 'But ... my birthday's tomorrow.'

'It is tomorrow! It's half three in the morning, your birthday's started already and what are you doing? Just lazing around.' He grins. 'Listen, I know you've got school tomorrow. I'm going to let you get back to sleep. I just wanted to tell you, we're going to celebrate properly this year, yeah? I want you to invite all your friends here after school. I'll get a takeaway. What do you fancy? What's your favourite food?'

'I dunno – Chinese?'

'Chinese it is then. We'll get the takeaway banquet. I'll get some balloons and hats, too – all that stuff. We can play pass the parcel.'

'Pass the parcel?' she repeats, still half asleep.

He laughs. 'OK, OK, I know you're eleven. Too grown-up and sophisticated for pass the parcel. Whatever you want, though. You bring all your pals and I'll bring the goodies. Four o'clock sharp. Wear your glad rags.'

She studies his face. His eyes are shiny with excitement. 'Dad, where have you been? We haven't seen you for days.'

'I know, I'm sorry, sweetheart. I just got caught up with things.'

'There was no money.'

'What? I left some on the mantelpiece.'

She shakes her head.

'Oh, man, I'm sorry. I could have sworn I did. Look, I'll make it up to you. I told you our luck was changing and I was right. Dad had a big win tonight. It's all down to you. You're my lucky charm!'

She says nothing.

'Well, aren't you going to congratulate me?'

She looks down at the bed and he taps her again on the arm. 'Hello, Maxie! Can you hear me?'

She wants to go back to sleep, back to the sweet factory.

'Speak to me!'

She raises her eyes to his. 'You said you were turning over a new leaf.'

He sighs. 'Oh come on, Maxie, don't be like that. It is a new leaf. Did you hear what I said? I won. Lots of money. That's good news. That means a fresh start. Now we can get straight.'

Get straight. It's what he always promises. Max

isn't even sure what it means. She imagines them being lined up against rulers.

'Oh, Max, you've got to trust me sometimes. I'll show you. This little birthday party will be just the start. Come on, don't look so down. Man, if you could see your face – you look like a fish finger at the swimming pool.'

Her dad always comes out with expressions like this: 'like a spider with two gloves'; 'like a duck with a pacamac'; 'like a sausage with a penknife'. He attributes them to random, absent family members – 'just like my old dad used to say', or 'in the words of Uncle Ivan' or 'like my granny always told me' – but Max knows he makes them all up. And try as she might to resist, they always make her laugh. The smallest smile escapes on to her lips and her dad beams back at her.

'That's my Maxie.' He hugs her and she breathes in alcohol and aftershave and other people's cigarettes. She loves the smell. He lets go and looks at her seriously. 'Now, this is important. What do you want for your birthday? Whatever it is, tell me. I'll get it while you're at school.'

She looks at him and shrugs. 'Just take me to

the safari park sometime. They've got a baby rhino there.'

'Maxie, if you want a baby rhino, I'll buy you one!'

She laughs. Her dad is crazily generous when he has money, but he buys mad things. She thinks of the fluorescent pink teddy the size of a small car she had to leave behind in one of their moves.

'Don't buy me a rhino, Dad.'

'Alright. If you say so. Look, you better get some sleep now. Don't forget: invite all your little friends.' He kisses her goodnight and starts to leave the room.

'Dad?'

'Yeah.'

'It might be a bit short notice for all my friends. I mean, they'd have to ask permission and all that.'

'Ask them anyway, I bet they'll come.'

Chapter Nine

Being a learning mentor has been more of a challenge than I thought. This is not because Max doesn't want my help like I thought. It's because Max doesn't need my help. Max doesn't need anybody's help. I'm beginning to think that Max might actually be some kind of genius. She can definitely do long division anyway, which makes her a genius in my book. To be honest, maths isn't my strong point. I find numbers as slippery as ice cubes in a glass of Coke. It's a real worry, because people who are exceptionally good at maths often go on to become evil criminal geniuses, so it's not completely out of the question that, one day, I'll need to be able to multiply fractions to solve a crime. But, then again, a calculator is one of the thirty-six functions on my watch so I'll have to rely on that.

Anyway, on Monday I was sitting trying to work out 3786 divided by 235, when I had a breakthrough. I suddenly realised that the problem with long division sums is that they are too abstract.

3786 what?

235 what?

Numbers don't just exist on their own, dividing and multiplying by themselves! They are connected to things!

So I came up with a real-world situation: I imagined an enormous bucket of 3786 ping-pong balls which had to be shared equally among 235 people. (Yes, I know, 235 is an odd number and you can't have an odd number of people playing table tennis, but I thought maybe there could be a substitute in the event of any ping-pong-related injuries.) Anyway, I pictured myself standing with the enormous bucket, waiting to hand out the 3786 balls to a nice, neat queue of 235 players. But once I had that image in my head things started to go wrong. Surely that was going to be a lot of ping-pong balls for each person to hold, I thought, especially if they were already holding ping-pong bats. In my imagination, people started dropping the balls all over the floor and scrabbling around after them; people were picking up other people's balls; people were getting angry and hurling ping-pong balls and table-tennis bats quite violently at one another … and that was when I felt someone tapping at my elbow.

'Hmm?' I said.

It was Max: 'Your page is blank,' she said, tapping my maths book with her finger.

'It is, yes.' Her observation skills are pretty basic.

'Why's that then?'

'Because I'm thinking. Calculating. Long dividing.' I didn't like to go into the whole ping-pong disaster scenario.

'The answer is sixteen, with a bit left over.'

'Pardon?' I said.

'Eleven left over in fact. Sixteen remainder eleven.' I stared at her – she had actually picked up her pencil and was doing the sum in her own book, humming merrily to herself. 'Can't resist a little bit of maths,' she said cheerily. 'Long division's not difficult, you know. My mum taught me the best way. First off, forget this bus stop foolishness. I'll show you.'

'But…' I said.

She looked at me. 'What?'

'Well … I mean, I'm the learning mentor.'

'But,' she tapped the blank page again and whispered, 'you're not very good at maths, are you? Now,' she said, in her normal voice again, 'look at this…'

That was how it started. Turns out that, not only could Max do long division, she could also explain it better than any teacher ever has and now I can do it, too. Not just long division either. Whenever I see her doing nothing and offer some help, she never needs it; she already knows the answers. It must be something to do with how many schools she's been to. She told me she's been to hundreds. Well, maybe not hundreds, I lost count to be honest, definitely tens, though. I guess she learns something new at each one and now she basically knows everything! Except how not to get expelled. She never seems to learn that.

I lean over and ask her to remind me how you calculate the area of a circle when Josh Ryman suddenly marches up to the front of the classroom and bangs his fist on the desk. Naturally Miss Casey is off on a FBD. Everyone falls silent.

'That's more like it. I could teach Casey a thing or two about class control.' He leans back against the desk with his arms folded, a grin spreads across his face.

'As you'll all have seen,' he announces, 'or if not seen, then smelt, we have a new addition to Class 6B.'

There are a few snorts of laughter from some of Josh's gang.

'It's called Max, but I'm not sure what it is. A boy? A girl? Some kind of creature?'

Josh has clearly not forgiven nor forgotten Max's threat to turn him into a rat. I start to get a bad feeling in my stomach.

It's obvious that Josh Ryman is going to grow up to be some kind of criminal mastermind. He already has most of the necessary skills and attributes: a baby face, a mean streak, a gang of dim-witted henchmen. He needs to work on some kind of crazed laugh – an evil cackle to let out whenever he comes up with a diabolical new plan – but apart from that he's pretty much all set. One day, when we're both adults, we'll come up against each other in a big case and I'll defeat him with my powers of detection and deduction and he'll never trouble anyone again.

'Oi, you, Mason!'

Josh is looking straight at me. This was a bit sooner than I'd planned. I was hoping I'd be less scared of him when I grow up.

'What about you? You're sat right next to it. What do you say?'

I try giving a shrug.

'What's that? Tut tut, Lori, you don't do that when Casey asks a question. Come on, now. What is it?'

Everyone looks at me. My heart beats loudly. I do what I always do in difficult situations and try to imagine what Sylvie Clandestino would do. Miss Sylvie Eveline Clandestino is my all-time favourite fictional detective. I think of the time she was held by kidnappers. They tried to force her to reveal the location of her secret underground headquarters. Sylvie just smiled and said: 'You'll never make me sing.' Which didn't actually mean sing. Singing would have been a crazy thing to do at that point. 'Sing' is American cop slang for 'tell'. The point is that Sylvie was totally cool under pressure and all the time she was secretly using the transmitter watch she'd invented to send her location to Jim, her equally brave crime-fighter husband. My watch is excellent and has thirty-six functions (I may have mentioned that) but, frustratingly, they don't include an emergency transmitter or any kind of Josh Ryman-elimination button. He's still staring at me with his weird baby eyes.

'Well? Chop chop. Answer the question!'

I think of Sylvie. She wouldn't be scared by a bully like Josh.

'Max is a girl,' I say quietly.

'Wrong answer!' shouts Josh, slamming his hand down so loudly that it makes me jump.

'You!' Max sits like a statue with her head down. 'You're going to have to help them. They all seem confused. You need to come up here right now, face the class and tell them what you are.'

She doesn't move.

'It's OK, I'm here to help you.' Josh is talking in a creepily soft voice now. 'You don't know what you are either, do you? You're not one thing, you're not the other, you're not really anything. That's it! You're nothing! Well, that can be your name from now on, to help us all to remember. Come on now, Nothing, the rest of the class need to hear it from you. You need to come up here and tell them your name.'

'Don't go,' I whisper to her.

But Max stands and stretches lazily like a cat waking up. She walks slowly up to the desk.

A smile spreads across Josh's face. He loves to win. Max walks until she's face to face with him.

'No,' he says. 'You're facing the wrong way. Turn around. Face the class. Tell them what you are.'

We can't see Max's face, but we can see Josh's smile slowly fade and his face begin to turn red.

'Why are you smiling, you mental case?' he shouts. 'Do you think this is funny? You won't. Turn around right now and repeat after me: "I am nothing."'

Silence.

'Say it! "I am nothing."'

Max leans toward Josh. Her face moves closer and closer to his face. I think she's actually going to kiss him! Josh's eyes are fixed on hers. She stops with just a fraction of an inch separating their noses. The entire class is holding its breath and then, suddenly, and very, very loudly, Max shouts: 'Boo!' and Josh Ryman jumps about six feet in the air. There's a moment's stunned silence and then everyone laughs and laughs and laughs. Everyone except Josh. He twists his angry, red face from side to side, glaring furiously, disbelievingly, at everyone laughing. When the laughter dies down, Max looks him up and down and says, 'You're right, you are nothing and now everyone knows it.'

She saunters back to her seat, turns to me and whispers, 'Want to come to a birthday party tonight?'

Chapter Ten

'I didn't know you lived above Rooster Party!' says Lori, standing on the doorstep, as if this was something she should have known. She seems weirdly impressed. 'Are you troubled much by the anti-social behaviour?'

Max is puzzled: 'What anti-social behaviour? You know the roosters aren't really having a party, don't you?'

'I'm talking about the littering. In the street outside. Fast-food debris. Attracts rats, Nan says.'

'Oh, that. Well, what's wrong with rats? They've got to live, too, haven't they?' says Max. 'Do you want to come in?'

Upstairs in the flat, Max can see that her mum has made an effort. She has changed out of her dressing gown into her jeans. She's set the table and put some crisps and kola kubes in little bowls. Best of all, she's also bought a big bottle of Dandelion and Burdock, which is Max's favourite.

'You ever tried Dandelion and Burdock

before, Lori? It's a bit old-fashioned but Maxie loves it,' says Max's mum.

Lori shakes her head. 'My nan is a bit anti old-fashioned things. She likes to keep up to date.'

'Ha. Does she? Good for her. Well, try a bit anyway; see what you think. The problem with liking old stuff is that it's not very easy to get hold of. I had to go all the way to Meacham's sweet shop to get this, that's the only place that still sells it. Still – it's for a special occasion isn't it?'

Lori takes a sip and Max can see straight away that she doesn't like it. 'Mmm,' she says 'Things really tasted different in the olden days. Could I have a glass of water, please?'

Max can't understand how anyone would ever choose to drink water, unless they were shipwrecked on a desert island and literally dying of thirst. She likes sugar in her drinks. The more sugar the better. Whenever they have squash at home, her mum always wonders how they get through it so quickly because she hasn't realised that Max likes to drink it undiluted.

While Max's mum is in the kitchen, Lori hands Max a gift and says, 'Happy birthday.'

Max looks at it. It's really nicely wrapped, like

the proper presents you see in shop windows at Christmas, with a ribbon and bow. She opens it carefully and finds a book.

'I don't know if you've read it already,' says Lori.

Max studies the cover. It's just a black front door. 'Sherlock Holmes,' she reads out loud. 'He's on telly, isn't he? Is he good?'

'He's amazing! He basically smokes a pipe, wears a big hat and solves crimes. He's super-clever but is best friends with a doctor called Watson, who is sort of the opposite. I mean not actively stupid, but definitely not a very bright person, but then again, he is cheerful while Sherlock Holmes is quite miserable, so you know, swings and roundabouts. If you like this, I can give you loads more. I'd also recommend Miss Marple. She's another brilliant detective. She lives in a place called St Mary Mead, which is a tiny village with an absolutely unbelievable amount of crime.'

Max isn't sure what to say to all this so tries: 'I've got a book about animals.'

But Lori hasn't finished yet. 'My favourite fictional detectives are actually The Clandestinos.

They're a married couple, Jim and Sylvie, and they're super-rich, so everyone thinks they just spend their lives swanking about in their enormous, luxury house in the California hills but, behind the scenes, the Clandestinos are totally dedicated to fighting crime. They have an entire underground HQ full of detective equipment. Jim Clandestino is amazing at disguises and Sylvie is brilliant with computers and technology.' Lori pauses for breath and then out of the blue asks, 'Max, have you ever wondered where Miss Casey goes during her Frequent Brief Disappearances?'

Max blinks. 'Her what?'

'When she's missing from class.'

'Miss Casey?'

'Yes. Where do you reckon she goes when she "pops out"?'

Max frowns. 'Well, she's at the photocopying machine. The barcode on her photocopying card has faded and the machine takes ages to register it, so it always takes her loads longer to get all her copying done than it should.'

Lori looks sceptically at Max. 'How have you deduced that?'

'Juiced what?'

'How did you work it out?'

'I didn't, she told me. I was late one day and I passed her in the corridor and she said, "Oh, Max, this machine will be the end of me," or something teacher-ish like that and then she told me about all her troubles with the card. She went on for ages about it. I didn't really know what to say, so I just offered to carry some of the copies back for her.'

'Oh,' says Lori.

'Why? What did you think it was?'

'Well, it just seemed a bit more mysterious than that.'

Max thinks for a minute and then says, 'Alright then. I've got one for you. What's Cheetham up to in the bike sheds?'

'Up to? Mr Cheetham? He's not up to anything. He's the caretaker. He's taking care of them. Cleaning them. Fighting grime.'

'Cleaning them?'

'Yes.'

'Up to seven times a day?'

'Well, evidently they get very messy.'

'Point one: do they look as if they have been cleaned seven times a day?'

'Well, it's hard to say.'

'Even once a day? Even once a week?'

'Well, maybe not, but the wind does blow a lot of litter back in.'

'Point two: does Mr Cheetham take cleaning tools with him into the sheds?'

'Cleaning tools?'

'Brushes? Dustpans? Bin bags?'

'Erm … actually now I think of it, no, he doesn't. I guess he keeps them in there.'

'Point three: have you ever seen Mr Cheetham's fingers?'

'His fingers?'

'Yes, his fingers. They're attached to his hands.'

'Yes, I know where his fingers are, and, yes, I've seen them.'

'But you've not noticed anything unusual about them?'

'Oh my goodness, does he have too many?' says Lori excitedly.

'What? No! He doesn't have too many. It's the colour. They're yellowy-brown. Right hand, these two fingers.' Max waggles her fingers at Lori.

'So?'

'Point four: do you ever see smoke coming from the bike sheds?'

'Actually, yes. Yes I do, sometimes, just a little bit.'

'And?'

'Well, I assume he burns litter in there sometimes. Maybe very, very small quantities of leaves.'

'Wrong! Mr Cheetham is a smoker. He's heavily addicted. His fingers are stained with nicotine. He can't get through the day without several cigarettes, so he tries to hide his anti-social habit in the bike sheds where he thinks no one can see him.'

Lori is completely silent for what feels like a long time and then says simply: 'Wow!'

'Wow what?'

'You're like a real detective. Like Sylvie Clandestino.' She hesitates and then says, 'Max, can you keep a secret?'

'Yes.'

'Well, guess what ... I'm actually a detective.'

Max looks at Lori closely. 'Aren't they normally taller?'

'Well, I mean, I'm training to be one. It's what I want to be when I grow up, so I'm practising now.'

'Oh! So that's why you carry that notebook everywhere in your pocket?'

Lori is astonished. 'How do you know about my top-secret notebook? You're incredible!'

Max grins. 'Well, that's true, but also you're not so great at hiding things. You're always writing in it.'

Lori's face falls. 'Sometimes I think I'm closer to Doctor Watson than Sylvie Clandestino.'

The conversation dries up and Max realises that she is very hungry. She has only eaten two kola kubes since lunchtime. Her mum has dozed off on the sofa again. Max notices Lori looking at the table set for dinner: the pink paper serviettes on the plates.

'Are we waiting for someone else to come?' Lori asks.

Max looks at the clock and sees for the first time how late it is. It's five o'clock, a full hour after he said he'd be there. She feels her mood drop instantly. Another broken promise. She should be used to it. She realises Lori is still waiting for an answer. 'No one else is coming,' she says.

'Oh. Right,' says Lori.

Max doesn't know what else to say, so she goes and fetches Lori's coat and hands it to her. 'You should probably go home.'

Lori looks confused. 'OK.' She looks again at the table set out for dinner. 'Are you sure we weren't supposed to be having some food?'

Max leads her to the door.

'I wasn't sure what happened at parties anyway. They always seem to have food at the ones on telly but Nan says you can't believe everything you see on TV. Well … thanks for … erm … the water. See you tomorrow…'

'Bye, Lori.'

Max closes the door behind her, goes into her room and lies on the bed listening to the clock tick. Sometime after seven her mum wakes up and looks in on her.

'You tired, sweetheart?'

Max says nothing.

'Your friend gone home? She seemed nice. We'll have to have her over again. Did I miss Dad? Did I miss all the food?'

Max squeezes her eyes closed.

'Sorry I dozed off, love. I don't know why I'm so sleepy all the time.' She sits on the bed next to Max and puts her arm round her shoulders. 'Happy birthday, Maxie.'

Chapter Eleven

Mr Wilson, the headteacher, is doing one of his assemblies. Mr Wilson loves stories with a moral. It doesn't bother him that these stories are generally totally unbelievable. Last week he told us a very long, rambling tale about some people who made soup from a stone! I have no idea where he gets these tales from. I think maybe he has an enormous book called, 'Unrealistic and confusing stories for children … ideal for assemblies!'

Anyway, amazingly, today's story is actually good. Apparently, it's an old Indian folk tale, but it's basically a detective story. It's about a rich man whose money is stolen from a locked trunk in his house. The only people with access to the trunk are his four servants so it has to be one of them but, of course, they all deny it. So the rich man asks the emperor (who also happens to be a part-time detective) for help. The emperor visits the four servants and says that as none of them have owned up he's going to have to use his magic sticks to find the thief. He shows them four identical sticks and tells them to take one each and sleep with it beneath their pillow. He says that the stick taken by the thief will magically grow two inches overnight, proving their guilt. That night the servant who actually stole the money reckons he can outwit the emperor and the magic detector-sticks by secretly chopping two inches from his stick so that, even when it grows, it will still look the same as the others. The next day when the servants show their sticks to the emperor the guilty servant is identified immediately. 'Aha! The sticks were not magical at all,' says the emperor. (I've added in the 'Aha!' as it sounds like the kind of thing an emperor would say when he got excited.) 'But your guilty conscience made you chop your stick, making it shorter than the others and revealing your guilt!'

Kapow! Just like that! Mr Wilson says the moral is that a guilty conscience will always be discovered. Though I think it probably helps a lot if the guilty party is a bit stupid, too, and has very little idea about the physical properties of sticks.

Back in class, Cuddles the hamster is making his usual racket. Cuddles is the most misleadingly named animal of all time. Cuddles doesn't like being cuddled. Cuddles doesn't like being touched. Cuddles doesn't even like being looked at. Cuddles mainly likes legging it round and round in his wheel, throwing himself at the bars of his cage and biting anyone crazy enough to put their fingers anywhere near him. Cuddles pretty much hates everybody except Josh Ryman, who as a consequence is permanent Hamster Monitor. Cuddles and Josh get along just fine, because Cuddles is basically just Josh in hamster form.

I'm returning from a pencil-sharpening expedition to the bin when I first sense that something is not right. I stop in the middle of the classroom trying to work out what it is.

'Are you alright, Lisa?' calls out Miss Casey.

'Hmm?' I scan the room.

'Are you quite alright? You seem rather lost.'

Then I see it! I keep my eyes on the spot and speak slowly. 'Have you taken it, Miss Casey?'

'Taken what, dear?'

'Did you take it to count? To check how close we are to the target?'

'Count what? I've done nothing but photocopy all breaktime, I'm afraid.'

71

'The money from the "Christine Aisley Dream Come True" collection box, Miss. It's gone.'

Suddenly everyone's talking and shouting and, for once, Miss Casey doesn't even bother trying to clap, but instead actually climbs up on her desk and shouts louder than she ever has, 'Silence! Nobody move from their seat.'

She gets down and walks over to the empty plastic box on the wall. The padlock hangs open. She takes her keys from her pocket and looks at them.

'Someone has removed the key to the padlock from my key ring.' She looks around the class slowly. 'Children, this is a serious matter. A large amount of money has been taken. I can't bring myself to think that any of you would have done this but, if one of you did, the time to speak is now, before this goes further. Maybe it was a dare. Maybe it was a joke. Whatever the case, we can help. I perhaps should remind you that this money is for Kieron's sister, a very seriously ill girl. If anyone has any information about this theft: speak now.'

The room is silent, no one moves. Miss Casey waits and waits. The clock ticks. Eventually, she turns to me and says in a quiet voice, 'Lisa, go and fetch Mr Wilson.'

Mr Wilson comes, then the deputy head, Mrs Hafiz, and then Mrs Garvey, the school secretary, joins in, too. Mrs Hafiz and Mrs Garvey check the cloakrooms and toilets and Mr Wilson and Miss Casey carry out a search of our bags and desks. After they finish, Mr Wilson speaks to us.

'Well, Class 6B. This is a very sorry day indeed. Despite our best efforts we have not found the missing money. And, despite our urgent enquiries, no one appears to be willing or able to shed any light on this disappearance.' He gives a little cough. 'Miss Casey, it seems, cannot be completely clear about when the key might have gone missing.' Miss Casey sits with her head bowed in the corner of the room. 'Miss Casey often leaves her keys on her desk as she has never had any reason to distrust anyone in the school.' He looks slowly around the room. 'This has been a painful lesson for her and many of the rest of us, I'm sure. I must ask you one last time, children, does anyone have anything they want to say?'

There's a long, unbearable silence and then, to gasps of disbelief, Lauren Pettigrew raises her arm.

'Lauren,' Mr Wilson says gravely, 'what is it you want to tell me?'

Lauren has tears running down her face. 'Mr Wilson, sir, are we all going to prison?'

'No, Lauren, all of Class 6B is not going to prison.'

But Lauren has opened the floodgates. Now lots of hands go up and Mr Wilson is inundated with questions and comments. None of them, it soon becomes apparent, are in any way relevant to the investigation.

'Will the school trip be cancelled?'

'Someone stole my pencil sharpener in Year 4.'

'There's a Chinese takeaway on my street called Great Wall of China – maybe we could take Christine there instead.'

'I can't find my trainers.'

'Will Miss Casey be sacked?'

Eventually, Mr Wilson calls order.

'That will be enough for now, Class 6B. I appreciate that this is a distressing time for all of you but the facts remain: a large sum of money has gone missing. We don't know who took it or even when. In the absence of anyone having any specific answers to those questions, I have no alternative now but to return to my office and call the police.'

Chapter Twelve

Peggoty is a big, fat, furry white fluffball of a cat who lies on the doorstep of Meacham's sweet shop every single day so that she can soak up the afternoon sun. Max thinks Meacham's is the best thing about living in New Heath. It's the greatest sweet shop she's ever known. It's an old-fashioned kind of place with a bell on the door and that still sells sweets in jars. Mr Meacham wears a funny kind of long brown jacket, as if being a shopkeeper is a job that requires a uniform. All the kids from New Heath go to Meacham's every day. They say the shop's been there so long that Mr Meacham used to serve their mums and dads when they were kids, too.

Max goes along every day, even though she never has any money. She goes because she likes looking at the sweets in the window even if she can't have them and because Peggoty is the closest thing she's ever had to a pet. She likes to sit on the step and talk to the cat in a low voice, telling her about her day. She rubs behind her ears and makes her purr her low, growly purr. Sometimes Mr Meacham has even come out and given Max a little striped paper bag of peanut brittle or pear drops. The first time he did it, Max was embarrassed. She said she'd forgotten her purse and couldn't pay, but Mr Meacham said the sweets were payment for looking after Peggoty.

Max is tickling Peggoty's tummy when Lori comes out of the shop and sits down next to her.

'Coconut mushroom?'

Max takes one. 'Thanks.' She chews for a moment, lost in thought. Finally, she seems to make up her mind. 'Lori, there's something I want to tell you.'

'Is it to invite me to another party? Only Nan said it's quite unusual to have no food and be back home forty-five minutes after arriving, so if it's going to be like that can you let me know so that I have some tea before I come.'

'It's not another party.'

'OK.'

'It's sort of to do with that, though.'

Lori gets up. 'Can we walk? The cat makes me sneeze.'

Max gives Peggoty a final rub and then gets up and falls into step alongside Lori.

'Well … so … the first thing you need to know is that I've never been expelled from a school in my life.'

Lori turns to look at her. 'What do you mean?'

She shrugs. 'Not once.'

'But you've been to loads of schools. I've lost count of the ones you've mentioned.'

'Yeah, I definitely have. But I was never expelled. We just always move on.'

'Why? Why do you keep changing schools?'

'It's not just schools. We move area, city, town, house, flat.'

'Oh, are you travellers? Shouldn't you have a caravan?'

'No, we're not travellers. We haven't got a caravan. Do you know what gambling is?'

'Yes, course. It's like the lottery, the Grand National, that kind of thing. Like my nan playing bingo sometimes.'

'Yeah, that kind of thing. Forget about the lottery and bingo, though. Horses maybe sometimes, dogs sometimes, but mainly cards. I'm talking about my dad, you see. My dad likes to gamble. Or maybe he doesn't like it, but he does it anyway, all the time. I don't know why because he's really rubbish at it. He gambles a lot and he loses a lot and then he borrows money and then he can't pay it back and then he gets scared of the men he's borrowed the money from and he wakes us in the middle of the night and tells us to put all our stuff in a bin bag because we're going to live somewhere new.'

'What? He runs away?'

'Of course he does.'

'Do the men ever catch him?'

'Twice. Once he was lucky. He'd just had a big win when they found him and he gave them everything. It was three times what he owed them, but they took it all … and our car, which was an old banger but still…'

'And the other time?'

'Not so lucky. He was in hospital for a long time. He's had a limp ever since.'

Lori's eyes are wide. 'What did the police say?'

'You don't go to the police, Lori. You're not allowed to tell tales. If you tell on the bad men … well … things get worse.'

'But what about your mum? Why doesn't she stop him?'

'She can't stop him. He has to stop himself. Anyway, she's not well.'

'Oh, sorry. What's the matter with her?'

Max sighs. 'I don't know really. She just has a lot of bad days. Gets depressed. Not like a bit sad-depressed, more like she can't move or do anything. Dad's always giving her pills. He says they make her feel better but they just make her sleep all the time. She's too ill to work. He collects all her benefits. Sometimes I think he actually likes her being sick because he gets her money. My dad scrounges and steals off everyone.' She kicks a stone along the road. 'That's why there was no party. No takeaway. He gambled all his winnings away again. He made a promise but he broke it. That's what he does.' She takes a deep breath. 'I just didn't know how to explain it all last night.'

Lori's quiet for a while and then says, 'Why don't you tell Miss Casey? She's nice. She'd help.'

'No,' Max shakes her head furiously. 'No grown-ups. I'm serious. You've got to promise. That's why it's a secret. I'm fine. I can look after myself, but they'd take me away from my mum, get someone else to look after me and then who'd look after her? You can't tell anyone. Please.'

Lori looks at her for a while and then nods. 'OK. I won't tell. I promise.' They've come to a stop outside a big, old house. 'Anyway, this is where I live. I'd better go.' She starts walking up the path and then stops and turns back. 'Don't suppose you want to come in for a bit, do you?'

Lori's kitchen and dining room are bigger than Max's entire flat. There are pictures and books everywhere. Max wonders if this is what most houses look like. She's not been in many other people's homes. The only houses she's ever visited belonged to her dad's mates, and they weren't really mates – just people he owed money to. Max doesn't have any grandparents but Lori's nan is definitely not how Max ever imagined nans to be. She wears a bright-pink baseball cap while she cooks. It says 'Party Girl' in diamante on the front. Max likes her. For tea she makes them spaghetti Bolognese followed by banana splits, with three flavours of ice cream. And squirty cream. And cherries and almonds. Max thinks Nan might be one of the finest chefs in the world.

After tea they go up to Lori's room – or her office as she calls it. Max gets a shock when she opens the door. Everything in the room is painted the colour of custard.

'Wow!' says Max. 'Is this what all detective's offices look like?'

'Not exactly,' says Lori. 'Try and imagine a different colour scheme ... and no rainbows ... or unicorns.' She walks over to her desk and pulls out what looks like two phones.

'These are genuine detective equipment, though.'

'What? Your nan lets you have a phone?'

'No. She says I'm still too young. These aren't phones. These are Kommunicator 150 walkie-talkies. Nan got me them from a car boot sale. They have a range of three kilometres!'

Max can't help picking one up and pressing the button:

'Roger, Charlie, Foxtrot. Calling Detective Mason. Do you read me, Mason?'

'Reading you loud and clear, Ellington, over.'

'What do you use them for?' Max asks.

'Well, they're for surveillance operations, but I haven't had the chance yet. I haven't really got anyone to use them with, except Nan, and she just uses them to tell me my tea is ready, or ask if I've seen her glasses, that kind of stuff.' She pauses for a moment. 'Why don't you take one home? You can do surveillance on New Heath high street and keep me posted on Rooster Party anti-social behaviour and local wrongdoing in general.'

'Are you worrying about the litter again?'

'Crime always starts small, Max. You begin by dropping litter, you end up involved in international diamond smuggling.'

Max grins and winks. 'Alright, I'll keep them peeled.'

She puts the walkie-talkie in her pocket and pulls out her snake charm.

'What's that?' asks Lori.

'It's my lucky charm.'

'A snake? Lucky?'

'Yeah! Very. You ever heard of the Scarlet Kingsnake?'

Lori shakes her head.

'They live in America. They're non-venomous. Harmless. Just these defenceless, dangly things that any other mean snake or bird can kill and eat whenever they want. But nobody picks on the Scarlet Kingsnake, because they look like the most poisonous snake you ever saw.

They're red and yellow and black like a big warning sign shouting, "Danger. Keep Away!" It's all just an act. But it works.'

'Oh … right,' says Lori.

'See, I used to go to this school. Addington Road it was called and it was a dump. The kids there didn't like me. Said I was dirty. Said I had fleas. Stupid songs and rhymes every day. Thing is – they were right. I was dirty. We didn't have a washing machine in the flat so I'd have to try and get money off Dad for the launderette and that wasn't always easy. It's not like I wanted to be that way. But, anyway, I got picked on. Punched and kicked sometimes. I was so glad when we had to run away from that place, but then I knew the next school would be the same and the one after that and that I was always going to be that girl. The one everyone laughed at or punched. And that's when I read about the Kingsnake.

'After that I stopped hiding in corners hoping no one would notice me. I didn't bother trying to hide the fact that my hair wasn't clean. No point. Everyone saw through all that. Instead I'd make it look so mad it was scary. And I wouldn't say, "Oh poor me – I had to leave my last school, I've got no friends." I'd tell everyone I was expelled, because I was the meanest, baddest girl around. And now maybe some people might still call me names, and they might talk about me behind my back, but they keep out of my way and they don't dare lay a finger on me. Nobody messes with Max Ellington any more.'

Lori looks at her and a big smile breaks out on her face. 'Max ... you're totally undercover. Just like me.'

Chapter Thirteen

Two police officers turned up after the theft. I was expecting blue tape across the classroom door; scene of crime officers dusting for fingerprints; I thought we'd at least all be questioned and tape-recorded, maybe even given lie detector tests. I wondered if some senior police officer might even pick up on my evident expertise and ask me to help with the investigation. But nothing at all happened. It was very disappointing. Then, this morning, Mr Wilson calls me into his office.

'Lori,' he says – he's quite good at remembering names – 'Miss Casey tells me that you are the only member of class who is absolutely sure that the money was in the collection box on Tuesday morning.'

'Yes, sir.'

'How can you be so sure?'

'Because I saw it, sir.' This seems obvious to me, but he nods as if it's, in fact, a very interesting answer.

'The thing is, Lori, sometimes it's hard to know exactly when we see things. Especially things that we see every single day. Sometimes we can be very sure we've seen something, but really we just assume that we've seen it, because we always do. Does that make sense?'

'Yes, sir. That happens to my nan all the time. The other day she was sure she'd seen her green bobble hat – she has bobble hats in a range of colours – hanging in the porch, because that's where she normally keeps it. But later on Mrs Evans brought it round, 'cos Nan had left it at her house and Nan hadn't even noticed!' I shake my head at the memory. 'Nan often mislays things.'

'Right. Well. Exactly, Lori. That's what I'm talking about. Very easy to get these things muddled up. So do you think that might have happened?'

'When, sir?'

'With the collection money. Do you think perhaps you think you saw it yesterday morning because you normally see it there?'

It's only now I realise that Mr Wilson is doubting my reliability as a witness. Me! Of all people! Does he have any idea of how precise I am in my note-taking, of my attention to detail, my years of close TV cop-drama viewing? Well, no, obviously he doesn't as it's all top secret, but one day, when I'm an internationally famous detective, he's going to be very embarrassed about this particular conversation. He blunders on, though, unaware of all this.

'The thing is, Lori, the fact that there was no trace of the money found in anyone's bag or desk or anywhere in the cloakroom, suggests strongly to the police that the money was taken out of school sometime before yesterday. A lot of people have been in and out of the classroom in the last few days: other children; the occasional parent; cleaners. Any one of whom might have seen Miss Casey's keys lying around and spotted an opportunity.'

Cleaners! Bad detectives always blame the easy suspect first – the cleaner, the maid, the butler. It's a textbook mistake. No, I decide, this can't go on.

'Mr Wilson, the money was definitely in the collection box yesterday morning. I know this because I check the box every morning when I arrive in class.'

'You know it?'

'I absolutely know it, sir.' I give him my hard-cop stare which I've practised in the mirror but which is unfortunately quite similar to my 'I desperately need the toilet' face. Mr Wilson doesn't seem to notice anyway.

'Well, Lori, I appreciate your help and, of course, it was you who noticed the money missing in the first place, so you clearly are an observant girl. I will certainly tell the police of your strong conviction that the money was there on Tuesday morning, but … I'm afraid, without concrete proof, they may have to stick to their current theory.'

Back in the classroom, no one seems fully awake. The heating's on full blast and I keep reading the same question on my worksheet over and over without taking it in. Suddenly Cuddles the hamster pipes up and breaks the silence. Cuddles has not been his demented self recently. He hasn't been on his wheel, hasn't been hurling himself against the bars of his cage, hasn't even bitten anyone for days. Now he lets out a long, sad-sounding groan, as if he just can't take any more. As if he hates the overwhelming heat and stupid fractions as much as I do. I almost feel sorry for him. It's only then that I notice Miss Casey crouching by Max's side.

'Maxine, could you open your desk, please?' she says in a very quiet voice.

Unfortunately, Max is off somewhere in Max-world and doesn't appear to have noticed Miss Casey's presence. I give her a gentle nudge.

'Hmm? What is it?' Max turns to me, blinking rapidly as if I've just woken her.

'Miss Casey wants you.'

She looks up at the front of the class and then turns back with a grin.

'She's not there. Off on one of her Frequent Brief Disappearances, ha ha!'

At this, Miss Casey clears her throat, making Max, who somehow still hasn't noticed her crouched at her side, jump quite dramatically, which makes everyone sitting nearby laugh and causes the whole class to turn their attention to what was clearly intended by Miss Casey to be a strictly hush-hush operation.

Miss Casey gives up on the soft voice and speaks normally. 'I'm sorry if I made you jump, Max. Could you please open your desk?'

'Why?'

'Could you just lift the lid, please?'

Max considers this for a moment. 'Are you searching me?'

'Yes, I'm afraid I am.'

'Is this about the money? Do you think I took it?'

'No, Max. I don't think that. I very much doubt we'll find the missing money in your desk especially as we've already searched all the desks once, but a certain accusation has been made, information given, anonymously, I might add, which is rather cowardly, and I hope to prove that accusation wrong.'

Max takes this in and then looks straight at me. 'Whatever she finds, I didn't do it.' Which is a mad thing to say as obviously Miss Casey's not going to find anything. Then Max stands up and steps away from her desk. Miss Casey lifts the lid and the whole class is out of their seats, crowding around to get a good look.

'All of you back to your seats!' Miss Casey shouts. 'You are supposed to be finishing your fractions worksheets. Anyone out of their seat will be sent to Mr Wilson.'

Everyone groans and drags themselves back to their chairs. Everyone except Josh Ryman who, I notice, never left his.

Miss Casey lifts the lid slowly and, of course, there's no big pile of money sitting inside. Instead there's a single maths textbook, a couple of exercise books and a Miss Marple paperback. Miss Casey seems quite relieved.

'Well, now, just as I thought. Nothing at all out of the ordinary here.' She moves the books from side to side as if to make a show of searching. 'Max, you can come back to your desk now and I'm sorry we had to do this, but...' She stops talking. Something slides from between the pages of the Miss Marple book and catches the light, glinting like a small dead fish at the bottom of the desk.

Max looks over Miss Casey's shoulder. 'What's that?'

'It's in your desk, Maxine. Shouldn't I be asking you that?'

'I haven't got a clue. It's not mine.'

Miss Casey sounds sad. 'No, it's not yours. I know that. It's mine. It's the key to the padlock that went missing from my key ring.' She's muttering to herself now. 'Easy to miss last time. Of course we weren't even looking for the key. No wonder we didn't see it.'

Max taps Miss Casey on the shoulder to get her attention. She looks her in the eyes and speaks slowly. 'Miss Casey, I didn't take your key.'

Miss Casey looks at her. 'Maybe you didn't, Max, but I'm afraid as it's been found in your desk, you're going to have to come along with me to see Mr Wilson and answer a few questions.'

Max's face hardens. She shrugs. 'Suit yourself.' And she follows Miss Casey out of the room.

All afternoon I wait for Max to come back but she doesn't. I keep thinking about her desk. I'm missing something, I know. A clue. A sign. I concentrate hard and try to picture in my mind exactly what I saw. A maths textbook. A couple of exercise books. The key sliding from between the pages of the novel. It's not until I'm putting my coat on at home time that my brain fog suddenly clears and I see it. The book! I run back into the classroom and catch Miss Casey before she leaves.

'Miss Casey!'

'What have you forgotten?'

'Imagine if you had stolen that key...'

'Oh. It's about that, is it? I'm sorry, Lori. I know you and Max are pals. This must be hard for you.'

'But if you had stolen that key. What would you do with it?'

Miss Casey sighs. 'I don't know, Lori. What would you do with it?'

'I'd smuggle it out of school as soon as possible.'

'Yes, that sounds fair enough.'

'And the only way I'd keep it in school is if it was in such a safe hiding place, there was no chance that any one would ever find it or know that I had taken it.'

'Again, I think that sounds about right. But often when people do things that are wrong they don't necessarily think very clearly. They make mistakes. That's how the police catch them.'

'The book.'

'Which book?'

'*Miss Marple's Final Cases* – the one that the key was hidden in.'

'Yes.'

'It just hit me: I only lent that to Max yesterday.'

'Right.'

'So she can't have hidden the key in the book, because she didn't even have the book when the robbery happened.'

'Yes,' says Miss Casey slowly. 'But she could have put the key in the book after you'd lent it to her.'

'But why would she do that? Why would she keep it at school and move it from place to place? Why would she put it in a book that she was reading – and I know she was reading it as we were talking about one of the stories at breaktime – where it could fall out at any point? That isn't what a criminal would do. It just doesn't add up!'

Miss Casey smiles. 'You've really thought about this, Lori. Do you know what – you sound a bit like a detective yourself!'

Sometimes Miss Casey can be quite infuriating.

'Lori, look. I know Max does not have an easy home life. I don't know the full situation, but I can see from her school history that she has had a very unsettled time. We can sympathise and we can try to help her but we can't, I'm afraid, allow her to steal.'

'Do you think we can help? Will you try and

speak to her tomorrow, Miss? Try and find out if there's some way we could help, you know, so that she's less ... unsettled.'

'Well, I would, Lori, but I'm afraid in this case, that's not going to be possible.'

'Why not?'

'Well, Mr Wilson needs to discuss the matter of the missing money and Max's possible involvement with it at the next meeting of the school's governing board. Until a decision is made, Max is suspended from school. She won't be coming back tomorrow.'

Chapter Fourteen

When Max gets home, she finds her dad in the hallway, going through all the coats.

'What you doing?'

'Nothing. Just looking for my keys.' He frowns. 'Why are you back so early?'

'I'm suspended. Where's Mum?'

'Asleep. What do you mean suspended?'

'School thinks I stole some money.'

'What they talking about?'

She shrugs.

'What money anyway? Dinner money?'

'No. Charity money. £300.'

He stops fiddling with the coats and looks at her.

'Did you take it?'

Max meets his eyes and he shakes his head. 'Course not. Look, I've got to run like a bean. Got to see a man about a dog.' Max notices that he's sweating.

'Dad,' she calls after him.

'Yeah.' He's opening the door. His hands are shaking. She wants to ask him if he's OK. To tell him to stay home. To come and read a book about animals with her, but instead she shakes her head. 'Nothing.'

'Suit yourself. Later potata,' he says and goes.

Max's dad is a superstitious man. He believes in black cats, four-leafed clovers, cracked mirrors and lucky horseshoes. He says that Max is his lucky charm. He always tweaks her nose for luck. And this is proof to Max of just how hopeless a case her dad really is, because it's clear that she brings him no luck at all. She used to actively wish him bad luck, in the hope that if he lost, he'd give up gambling for good. But now she knows it doesn't matter what he loses: TVs, cars, jewellery, houses. He always goes back.

Max might think her dad crazy for believing that she could ever bring him luck, but she's just as superstitious as him. She has total faith in the power of her snake charm. It's old and heavy, solid silver with green gems for eyes. It was once her mum's. 'Keep it safe,' she said when she gave it to Max, meaning: 'Don't let him get it.' And Max doesn't. She keeps it in her pocket and whenever she feels it there, she knows that she and her mum will get through it all.

The next morning, Max is surprised to find her mum up before her. She gives Max a hug and then notices the time.

'Hey, why aren't you at school yet, Maxie?'

Her mum's always better in the mornings: brighter, more focussed. Max can tell a lot from her mum's eyes. Sometimes, even when they're open, it's like they are closed: not really registering anything. The first time Max heard about driverless cars it made her think of her mum: moving about, lights on, but nobody really there. Today though, her eyes look different, some spark or light that makes it seem as if a real person is actually inside. Max never lies to her mum, but she can't face telling the truth about school and risk making that spark vanish.

'It's a teacher-training day.'

'Nice. Have you seen the sky this morning? Look at it! Not a cloud. Solid blue.' She looks out of the window and then turns to Max. 'Hey! Why don't we go for a walk?'

'You want to go out?' Max is amazed.

'Yeah. I really do. I'm sick of sitting in this place all the time. I want some air. A woman needs to breathe sometimes, you know.'

Max smiles. 'We could go feed the ducks in the park.'

'Ducks! Man, when was the last time I saw some ducks? Not since you were a crazy little chubby thing, chasing them with your chocolate buttons.'

'Those ducks loved me.'

'Yeah, that's why they used to run away. Come on, let's do it. But first I need some coffee and we're out of milk. Could you run and get some?'

'Sure.' Max grabs her jacket and her backpack and heads out. She'll buy some chocolate buttons as well, to make her mum laugh.

Out on the street it's a bright, crisp day. Everything looks clean and fresh, even the pavement outside Rooster Party. 'Spring has sprung,' thinks Max and she repeats that over and over in her head in time with her footsteps. She thinks about all the animals waking up after their long winter hibernation. Maybe that's what her mum has been doing for the last year or two –

kind of hibernating. Maybe, while she's bright and in a good mood, Max could persuade her to go and see a doctor. It can't be right to sleep so much.

Max is actually skipping, when a strange woman steps in front of her.

'Hey, Max! Slow down. I've been trying to catch up with you.'

Max looks her up and down. 'Do I know you?'

'Yes, love, I'm Julie. I'm a friend of your dad's. Don't you remember me?'

Max has met lots of her dad's gambling cronies over the years but she doesn't recognise Julie. 'Look, Max, your dad's in a bit of bother. He's asked me to come and get you. He needs your help.'

'What do you mean? What kind of bother.'

'Nothing serious. He just needs a favour.'

'Why doesn't he ask me himself?'

'Look, love, it's nothing to worry about. He's just tied up with something and asked me to come and find you.'

'But my mum's waiting for me. She needs some milk.'

'That's OK. Your dad'll ring your mum and explain. Don't worry, it's just a quick favour. Twenty minutes at the most.'

Max can guess what the favour will be. Now she's off school, he'll have her doing all his errands. She'll be sent to give messages and excuses to blokes he owes money to. He always tries that when things are bad. He thinks they'll go easier on a kid than on him. Max's instinct tells her to say no, to get back to her mum, but she knows her mum would want her to help her dad. She sighs. 'OK, twenty minutes max.'

They walk to a housing estate. The high-rise flats block out the sun on the ground and it doesn't feel like spring any more. A sharp wind blows around the bottom of the flats, making Max shiver. A lot of the tower blocks are empty, awaiting demolition. Some of the houses are boarded up, too. Julie leads them to a green front door at the end of an empty-looking row of houses.

'Here you go.'

'Here?'

'Yeah, come on, your dad's waiting.'

Max hesitates. 'What's he doing here?'

'He's just lying low, love. You know, keeping out of certain people's way. You know the kind of trouble he gets himself in.'

Julie unlocks the door and lets Max in ahead of her.

'He's upstairs, love, back bedroom. Think he said he might have a nap so you'll probably have to wake him up. You go on up. I've just got to grab something from the kitchen.'

Max heads upstairs and opens a door. The room is completely dark and she squints to make out her dad. She steps inside, waiting for her eyes to adjust.

'Dad?' she calls.

Suddenly the door bangs shut behind her and she hears a key turn in the lock.

'Hey!' She hammers on the door. 'Open up!'

'It's alright, Max, love.' She hears Julie's voice. 'You're alright. Your dad will be with you soon. Just locking the door for your own safety.' Max hears footsteps run down the stairs and a door slam.

She finds a light switch and turns it on. She sees now why the room was dark. The window is completely boarded up.

She suddenly remembers her dad looking through the coats the previous day. She reaches in her jacket pocket for her snake charm. It's gone.

Chapter Fifteen

'Aren't you going to finish your Coco Pops?' asks Nan. Rain's forecast for later in the day so Nan's fully prepared by wearing a yellow sou'wester fisherman's rainhood. In the kitchen.

I stare into the chocolatey milk. 'Hmm?'

'Your Coco Pops. You've hardly touched them.'

'No.'

'But you didn't eat your tea last night either. I bought potato smiley faces especially. I thought they'd cheer you up.'

I hadn't felt like eating. A plate of potato heads grinning up at me hadn't really helped.

'Look, I know you're sad about Max getting the blame. But not eating isn't going to help the situation.'

'She didn't do it, Nan. She's been framed.'

'I know, love. We've been through this and, for what it's worth, I don't think she did it either.'

'That evidence was planted.'

'Well, it's possible.'

'It's certain! No one at school knows how smart Max is. If she was going to steal money, she'd do it right. Her tracks would be totally covered. She's not an idiot. She wouldn't keep the key in her desk!'

'No, I know that, but if you don't hurry up and eat your breakfast, you're going to be late for school.'

I look at the spoon.

'Look, Lori, this is not like you – moping about. I thought you were a detective! I thought you wanted a crime to solve! Does Miss Marple starve herself when she's baffled?'

I think about it. 'No. She probably has an iced bun.'

'Exactly. Or a slice of fruit cake.'

'Or possibly a crumpet.'

'Of course she does! She feeds her brain. You need food to function properly. Now, listen to me, you're going to finish that bowl of Coco Pops in the next three minutes, then you're going to have a nice piece of hot, buttered toast to make up for missing tea last night and then you're going to go to school with that enormous brain of yours firing away on all cylinders and you are going to get to the bottom of this missing money nonsense! Are we agreed?'

Nan's right. What's the point of all my detective training and preparation if all I ever do with it is locate lost glasses and hats? Here I am, finally, with a proper case to solve: missing money, dodgy evidence, a friend wrongfully accused! I need to get to work.

As soon as I arrive at school I can sense it: something's not right. When I get to the classroom, Miss Casey looks pale and worried. She's waiting with the police officers. Detective Superintendent Alison Burrows gets up to speak to the class and tells us all that Max has gone missing.

Afterwards she leads me to an interview room that they've set up in the sick bay. I've never been in the same room as an actual real detective before. Alison Burrows is probably a brilliant investigator and normally the idea of being asked for help with an enquiry would be amazing, but it doesn't feel amazing today.

'Now, Lori, Miss Casey tells me you were probably Max's closest friend in the class. Is that right?'

I nod.

'When did you last speak to Max?'

'The day before yesterday, when she got suspended. I was going to call round for her tonight after school.'

'I see. Now, we know Max has enough money to get some distance away from New Heath. Have you any idea where she might have gone? Did she ever speak about somewhere special?'

I shake my head. 'Max hasn't got that money.'

'Well, the evidence seems to suggest she has.'

'No. There is no evidence. Someone planted the key in her desk. I told Miss Casey that. They searched all of us the day the money went missing. None of us had it. How could she have it now?'

'Well, we're not certain of the details yet.'

'You're not certain, because it's not true. Max hasn't got the money and she wouldn't run away.'

'I know she's your friend, Lori, and I know it's upsetting, but we all need to keep an open mind.'

I find myself standing up. 'My mind is totally open. If Max is missing, then something really bad has happened to her and you need to start investigating that and stop saying she stole some money and she's run away from home when it's obviously not true!' I've never shouted at an adult before in my life.

Detective Superintendent Alison Burrows says nothing. She looks at me for a long time and then stands up slowly and opens the door. 'Thank you, Lori. That will be all for now.'

Chapter Sixteen

Max can't tell how long she's been in the room. Maybe an hour, maybe two. There's a bed on the floor, a little child-size table with two chairs – and that's it for furniture. There is a door that leads through to a very small loo and shower room. The en-suite door is locked from the outside, too.

Max has been in scary situations before. One time, when she was little, some men came looking for her dad. Her mum was in the middle of reading a bedtime story when the hammering started on the front door. Max got scared and her mum held her tightly. She said, 'It's OK, Maxie, they can't get in.' But they kept banging and banging and shouting. So then she said, 'Maxie, we're going to play a game. We're going to go and hide and be as quiet as mice.' She carried Max into the cupboard and shut the door. Max remembers the sound of her mum's heartbeat crushed up against her ear in the darkness. Afterwards, when the men had finally left, her mum told her how good she'd been.

'It's not easy when you're scared. Makes you want to scream and cry, but now you know what you've got to do with fear, you've got to swallow it. Gulp it down, so it can't escape out your mouth.'

Max has got pretty good at swallowing fear since then. Once you've learnt the trick you can face down all kinds of troubles. She does it now as she hears a door slam downstairs. A few moments later Julie enters the room and locks the door behind her. She's smiling, like nothing at all has happened, and carrying a plastic bag.

'Got you some pop and crisps. Didn't know what flavour you liked, so I got a multipack.'

'Where's my dad? I want to go.'

'Why don't you sit down, have some crisps and we'll have a chat.'

'I don't want any crisps! I want to go. You said twenty minutes. You locked me in.'

Julie's smile fades. 'Well, I think that's just rude. Bit spoilt, in fact. I got you a multipack. So, you know, if you want answers to your questions, it would actually be a really good idea for you to sit down and listen. And try being a bit more grateful. This could turn out to be a nice holiday for you if you cooperate instead of acting up.'

Max thinks that the woman might be mad. Max hasn't been on many holidays in her life, but she's pretty sure they don't involve getting locked in boarded-up bedrooms. The woman starts fussing with the bags of crisps, laying them out on the table like they're about to have a party.

'Your dad's in a bit of trouble, do you know that?'

'My dad's always in trouble.'

'He owes lots of money to lots of people. Do you understand?'

It's as if the woman thinks Max is four years old.

'Course I understand.'

'He's sold the telly again, hasn't he? And the laptop. He's even sold his phone, but he still hasn't got enough money, so what do you think he should do?'

'I don't care. I don't want to talk about my dad. I don't want to eat crisps. I want to go home. If you don't let me out right now, I'm going to start screaming and look at my mouth: it's massive. I've got a really loud voice.'

'Go ahead and scream if you want. No one will hear you. But if you want to see your mum again, it'd be better if you played nice.'

This silences Max. She sits on the bed.

'That's better. Now, you haven't answered my question. What do you think your poor old dad should do?'

Max shrugs. 'Run away, I suppose. That's what we always do.'

'But he can't run for ever and anyway … maybe there's no need.'

'You said he was in trouble.'

'I did, but there's a way out of it. He's got something more valuable than the rest of all his other stuff put together.'

Max racks her brains trying to think of anything else they might have that's worth money. The only jewellery her mum has left is fake. 'What are you talking about?'

The woman smiles a horrible smile. 'I'm looking right at it.'

Max shoots up off the bed, but the woman is there with her hand on her shoulder, gently pushing her back down again.

'Now, Maxie, nothing to get scared about. The fact is you're a kid and people care about kids. They don't like them going missing. Everyone worries about a missing kiddie. It's just natural. They'll be looking for you soon.'

'Who are you? Have you ever even met my dad?'

'Oh yeah, I've met him lots of times. Let's just say I'm a friend of a friend. He talks too much, your dad. Did you know that? Especially about you. Always going on about you, he is. Maybe if he chatted less and concentrated more, he'd do better at cards, but there you go. I started thinking a while back that it was a shame he didn't see what an asset you are. That's when I hatched my plan.'

'A plan to kidnap me?'

'Hey! Less of that.' Julie seems offended. 'This isn't a kidnapping. This is a fake kidnapping.'

'You locked me in. How's that fake?'

'Look, this is a win-win situation. What happens when a kid goes missing?'

Max shrugs.

'Fine, I'll tell you. Some rich do-gooder steps in and offers a reward, that's what happens. They always offer a decent wad of cash to anyone who helps find the kid. And guess who's going to be the one to get this reward?'

Max splutters. 'Not you?'

'Yes, me. Course me. I'm going to find you, aren't I? Julie's going to be the hero for finding Max.'

'But you're the one who took me.'

'Oh no, nobody took you, love. You ran away from home. If the police think you've been kidnapped, there'll be too much heat, they'll be all over every inch of ground within twenty miles of New Heath. If they think you ran away – well, they'll still look for you, course they will, they'll still offer a reward, but it's a little less risky for me.'

'I would never run away from home.'

'Well, that was a bit of a problem for me. I wondered how I was going to make that look realistic. I mean your dad's always saying how close you are to your mum. Then last night came the break I needed. Your dad mentioned when he was playing cards how you'd been suspended for stealing all that money. Tut tut. Naughty Maxie.'

'I didn't take that money. Somebody set me up!'

'That's what your dad said: "As if my Max would ever steal a thing." Problem is, Max, that everyone else thinks that you would and that you did. Right now, everyone thinks you've run off somewhere with £300. And I'm going to be the one who finds you.'

'Your plan is stupid and you're stupid if you think I'd ever go along with it.'

113

'But you will, Maxie. Once I "find" you, you're going to tell the police exactly what I tell you to say: you ran away, you spent your money, you were sleeping on the streets when I found you and saved you. That way, I get the reward money. I keep half for coming up with the idea, and here's the best bit – you get half to give to your dad to pay off his debts and stop all those nasty men he owes from hurting him.

'If you go telling tales to the police, I'll tell them your dad was in on the plan, too, that he put me up to it, that he was the brains behind the whole thing. I don't think they'll like that.' She smiles at Max. 'Come on, admit it. It's perfect, isn't it? And can you see now how simple it is? I know you don't want to get your dad in trouble, so just make sure that when the time comes you stick to the story. I reckon that mouth of yours is good at making up all kinds of stories. Until then, all you need to do is sit tight and eat your crisps.'

Chapter Seventeen

"I have heard of you, Mr Holmes. I heard from Major Prendergast how you saved him in the Tankerville Club scandal."

"Ah, of course. He was wrongfully accused of cheating at cards."

"He said that you could solve anything."

It's the fifteenth time I've read the same three lines. I close the book and give up. It's hard to get wrapped up in some long-ago, made-up mystery when you find yourself slap in the middle of a right-now, real-life mystery.

One of the many bad things about Max going missing is that suddenly everyone in 6B reckons they're a detective. And when I say detective I don't mean Sylvie Clandestino or Sherlock Holmes, I don't even mean Doctor Watson on one of his slow days, I mean the kind of detective who doesn't really grasp the concept of evidence or clues, or even logic.

Dexter Foyle is convinced that Max has run off with the circus. Lucas Spiers reckons she's gone to Disneyland Paris or at least, he says, that's what he'd do if he had the money. Nina Masters 'has a feeling' that she's living on a narrowboat on the canal. Elijah Stephens thinks she may have been taken by aliens. Most people are sure she hasn't gone to the Great Wall of China. They all think it's exciting. 'What's she doing with all that money?' they keep asking. Everyone in 6B thinks Max is a crazy, rule-breaking outlaw on the holiday of a lifetime. Everyone except me. I know the undercover Max and I know she wouldn't run away and leave her mum behind.

Nan thinks something's wrong, too. When the six o'clock news finishes, she says, 'Why didn't Huw mention Max?'

Nan's on first-name terms with the newsreader, Huw Edwards. She's secretly in love with him. (She hasn't admitted this, but I've collected enough evidence in the form of comments regarding his 'lovely accent' and 'twinkling eyes'.) But she's not happy with him now.

'They should be making more of a fuss! She's eleven years old, for goodness sake. Why isn't she on the news?' Nan doesn't wait for me to answer. 'I'll tell you what I reckon: they don't think she's the right sort to make a fuss about.'

'What do you mean?'

'Look, love, I don't know anything about Max's mum, or her dad, but I know a hungry kid when I see one. I've never seen anyone eat so fast as when she had her tea here. Her clothes are too small for her and I'm afraid to say that they look like they need a good wash. I'm not standing in judgement and I certainly don't blame Max, but a fact's a fact: she's not being looked after properly, anyone with eyes can see that.'

I don't know what to say. I promised Max to keep her secret. But Nan doesn't need me to say anything anyway, she's on a roll.

'And now nothing about her on the news! It makes me cross, it does. It's as if they've decided she's not worth looking for. "Oh, she's probably run away," they say. "Probably trouble at home." Well, what's that got to do with anything? She's a young girl out there on her own. It doesn't matter if she's run away.'

'She hasn't, Nan. I'm sure of it!'

'Well, maybe she has and maybe she hasn't

but, either way, they should be making more of an effort! More of a fuss. She's eleven! She needs to be found and she's not going to be if no one knows she's missing! Well, I'm not sitting back and doing nothing! Are you?'

I shake my head. 'But what can we do?'

'Well, first thing in the morning, I'm going straight round to Ritzy.'

'Nan! Buying a new hat's not going to help.'

'Buying a new hat always helps, love, but that's not what I'm planning. They do T-shirt printing at Ritzy. I'm going to get a load of "Find Max" T-shirts printed up and hand them out at the school gates. Then I'm going to get on to my friend Marjorie, she can help us.'

'Marjorie? Mad Marjorie? The one who rides the micro-scooter and wears wraparound sunglasses?'

'She's not mad, love.'

'You always say she is.'

'OK, she's a little bit mad. But she's just what I need here. If I'm going to set up a campaign, I need help. Marjorie went to all the Silver Surfer sessions for OAPs at the library, she knows all there is to know about … you know … Tweety…'

'Twitter?'

'Yes, Twitter and the rest of that cyber...'

'Social media?'

'Social media! That's it! Social media ... stuff. She can be in charge of all that. I'm on a mission, Lori. There's not going to be a single person in this country who doesn't know Max's face when I've finished.'

Nan's right, we need to be doing more. I'm going to help all I can with the campaign, but there's something else I can do, too. The only way to get the police to realise that Max hasn't run off is to prove that she didn't steal the money. If I can do that, then maybe they'll start looking for her properly. I open my notebook and look for the hundredth time at the only solid, indisputable facts I have.

1   *Fact: the money was in the box on the morning of March 12*[th]

2   *Fact: the money was gone by lunchtime of March 12*[th]

3   *Fact: the only people with access to the box between those times were Miss Casey and the rest of class 6B*

4   Fact: everyone's coats, bags and desks were
    searched thoroughly as soon as the theft
    was noticed.

This all points to something but I can't quite work out what. It feels like I'm trying to reach a jar on a shelf that's a bit too high for me.

It's 2.28 a.m. when I'm woken up by the realisation. I sit straight up in bed, put on my light and reach for my notebook and pen. There can only be one answer and it's so obvious I've somehow missed it. I write in big, capital letters on the first clear page.

'MONEY STILL IN CLASSROOM!'

Chapter Eighteen

Although she can't see outside, the little daylight that escapes around the edge of the boards tells Max that she has been in the room for five days now. Where the room is, though, she still has no idea. She remembers a housing estate, and that it wasn't far from New Heath, but that's all. She can't get used to the silence. No buses rumbling past, no schoolboys shouting and throwing chicken bones at each other, just birds endlessly tweeting. No one seems to live on the estate, or even pass through.

Julie visits three times a day. She brings Max whatever food or drink she wants, along with comics and books and clean clothes. Max just gives her a list and she gets it. A bit like Father Christmas, thinks Max, but with a key. It's as if Julie thinks it's not really kidnapping if you buy someone sweets.

Today when Julie arrives bringing breakfast from McDonald's, she's beaming. 'Thank God for Mrs Pam Southwell.' She holds up a newspaper.

Max splutters. 'What is that?' The front page is covered with a photo of Lori's nan giving a thumbs up. She's wearing a baseball hat with a picture of Max's face on the front. 'Where did she get that hat?'

'Never mind that. Look at the headline!'

'£50,000 reward!'

'£50,000, Max! Don't you feel special? It's all down to that little old lady. I was beginning to think I'd made a bit of a mistake. The runaway story wasn't helping us at all. Nobody cared. Well, your mum, bless her, did her best in the local paper, but no one was really that bothered until Granny Hat here started up her "Find Max" campaign. It's tugged on the heartstrings of local business owner, Keith Barker, and he's stumped up all that cash.'

'Where did they get that picture of me? It's terrible!' In it Max is wearing a red V-neck jumper. She realises that it must be a forgotten school photo that her mum never bought.

'It's brilliant, isn't it. Look at those big, sad, brown eyes. You're like a lost puppy.'

Max has never been very good at smiling in photos.

'You watch, there'll be sightings of you all over the place now there's money around. "A girl fitting Max Ellington's description spotted in Hastings, …in Edinburgh, …in Paris." The police are going to be running all over the place.'

'So is it over? Can I go? You can get your reward?'

Julie shakes her head. 'Oh no. Julie's smarter than that.'

Max hasn't noticed Julie being especially smart but she says nothing.

'Nah. You claim the reward straight away and it looks fishy. It's got to look realistic, Max. We need to wait a few more days. Who knows? Granny Hat carries on the way she's going, they might even put the reward up!'

Chapter Nineteen

Sometimes detectives have to approach a case from the side – crab-style – and this is exactly what I'm doing. This is why I've been extensively researching hamsters, which to some onlookers might appear to be a waste of time and nothing whatsoever to do with finding Max. Some onlookers, however, would be wrong wrongington. My notebook now contains everything I know about hamsters.

1   *Hamsters do not even like other hamsters (let alone human beings).*
2   *Hamsters like to be alone. When put together they get stressed, aggressive and may even kill each other!*
3   *Hamsters can horde so much food in their cheek pouches that their heads may double or even triple in size!*
4   *Hamsters eat their own poo!*
5   *Hamsters are crepuscular, which means*

they are mainly active around dusk, which
means they are inactive for most of the time,
which means they are not very exciting pets.
Unless you are also crepuscular.

6   *Lady hamsters are even more aggressive*
    than men hamsters.

7   *Sometimes, if a lady hamster is in a really*
    bad mood, she will eat the man hamster
    after mating.

8   *If a lady hamster is disturbed whilst giving*
    birth, she might eat her babies. Some lady
    hamsters pretend that they were just trying
    to look after their babies in their cheek
    pouches when they accidentally swallowed
    them, but nobody believes them...

9   *...because regardless of being disturbed*
    during birth, if a lady hamster is left alone
    with her babies for more than three weeks,
    she will probably eat them anyway.

10 *Hamsters like privacy. <u>If hamsters do not</u>*
    <u>have a private shelter within their cage,</u>
    <u>they will become stressed and depressed</u>.

I've underlined the last item on the list several
times.

It's break time before I'm finally alone in the classroom. When I'm sure the coast's clear – after Elijah Stephens has been back for his jumper, then his asthma inhaler and then his tissues – I stop pretending to finish off my English comprehension and head straight for Cuddles' cage. I won't deny I'm nervous. I remember that normal hamsters eat their own babies. What will a psychopathic one do to my fingers?

I reach out very gently to open the cage and slowly, slowly inch my hand inside. Cuddles doesn't move. He really isn't the hamster he once was. Back in the old days he'd have leapt at the chance to give a nice juicy hand a good savaging, but now he just sits in a pile of wood shavings and watches sadly. My target is the little wooden house in the corner of the cage where he used to spend most of his time. I'm not sure what he actually did in there. Slept? Read? Plotted a global hamster takeover? I've neither known nor cared much. The only thing I do know is that he hasn't been in that house for some time.

I carefully lift Cuddles' little wooden house from the floor of the cage and inside is an Asda carrier bag: the kind Nan refuses to pay 5p for. I let out a small victory yelp. The bag's heavy and, when

126

I look inside, I see exactly what I'd hoped to see: a higgledy-piggledy jumble of notes and coins.

Now we have the bait, we need to set the trap. I go and find Miss Casey and tell her the news and the plan.

Miss Casey makes the announcement straight after lunch:

'Now, Class 6B, if you could settle down, please, I'm afraid I have some very sad news. Some of you may have noticed something missing from the classroom this afternoon.' No one has, a few heads now look around half-heartedly. 'I'm sorry to say that during lunch break it was discovered that our dear own little Cuddles had sadly died.' A murmur of surprise passes around the room. 'I think we've all noticed that Cuddles has not been himself recently and it seems that he has not been a well little hamster for some time.' Perhaps everyone in 6B is too preoccupied by Max's disappearance to get upset over a hamster that never seemed to like us very much, anyway. For whatever reason, no one seems too bothered by Cuddles' passing. No one, that is, except for Josh Ryman who gets really quite agitated.

'Miss! Miss! I'm Hamster Monitor. Why wasn't I told first?'

'Josh, it happened during lunch break and you were out playing. I decided to deal with the situation and tell the whole class together.'

Josh's hand's up again.

'But, Miss, where's the cage?'

'Oh, yes. Well, I'm afraid I had to be a little drastic there. When I found poor Cuddles, I noticed some strange, dark spots on his tummy. After a little research I discovered that Cuddles had contracted a very unpleasant hamster disease called *Spottitummitosis*. I'm afraid this disease is actually transferable to humans. It doesn't kill us, but it can lead to a nasty rash and so, I'm afraid, I have had to dispose of Cuddles' cage and everything in it.'

'*What*?' blurts Josh.

'I'm sorry, Josh. What was that?'

'I mean … how did you dispose of it, Miss?'

'Well, Josh, I understand that, as Hamster Monitor, this has all come as a bit of a shock to you and you must be rather upset. I don't really see the fact that I've put the cage in the large bin at the back of the school canteen is really a pressing concern of yours, though.'

Josh runs his hands through his hair and looks as if he might be sick.

After school Miss Casey says I can wait with her. We sit at one of the large empty tables in the canteen. It doesn't take long for a weirdly twitchy-looking Josh Ryman to creep up to the large dustbin outside. Miss Casey texts Mr Wilson as we watch Josh carefully lifting the bin's giant swing lid. He peers into the bin for a long time, moving his head from side to side. He climbs up to perch on the edge and uses a cardboard tube he finds to poke about inside. After a minute or two, something catches his eye and he leans in further and further to reach as far as he possibly can, until, finally, he stretches too far and falls in. The bin wobbles and the giant plastic lid falls, slamming shut with a big, echoey bang. When Josh emerges some minutes later, he has traces of egg shell in his hair, some banana peel on his arm and he's holding an empty Asda carrier bag. Mr Wilson is waiting for him, holding up a plastic folder filled with money.

'Is this what you were looking for, Josh?'

Chapter Twenty

If there's one thing that Max has learned from Lori and her detective books, it's that even the smartest criminals make mistakes and Max realised early on that Julie was not really in the smart criminals' league. It seems to Max that there are very obvious problems with Julie's so-called masterplan. After Max is 'found' the police are going to have lots of questions for her. Julie has told her to keep her answers vague. But Max knows that the police don't like vague; they like specific, they like detail, they like evidence. Where has she been all this time? Where exactly did she go when she left her house? Why hasn't she been spotted on CCTV? Where has she been sleeping? There's also the awkward question of her appearance. She doesn't look like a runaway. She's never had so many takeaways and sweets in her life. She'll be the first runaway ever to have gained weight.

Max misses home. She misses her *Wildlife Atlas of the World*. She misses hearing Lori's detective theories. She even misses the permanent smell of chicken fat. But most of all she misses and worries about her mum. She remembers how happy she seemed on that last morning. She knows it's stupid, but she keeps imagining her mum still waiting in the kitchen for her to come back with the milk.

She can't forgive her dad. Every time she looks at the boarded-up window or the locked door she blames him. Not because of his gambling, or his debts, or his lies, but because he took her snake charm. The one thing that had always kept her mum and her safe and he stole it for whatever money he could get. It won't be bringing him good luck, she feels sure of that.

In the long hours when Julie's not there, Max sits at the little table and tries to think of ways out, but her ideas never get past the locked door and the shuttered window. She makes a list.

Negatives:
Locked door
Boarded-up window
Don't know where I am
Everyone thinks I've stolen money and run away

Positives:
Julie's not very clever

It's not much to go on, but it's all she has. If Julie was clever, she'd have checked Max's backpack the first day she took her and found the Kommunicator 150 walkie-talkie Max now keeps hidden under her pillow.

'Come in, Lori. Lori Mason, can you hear me?'

Every night Max tries all the channels but gets nothing back. She keeps trying, though. Lori might not always be out of range. She might pass nearby. She might have her walkie-talkie with her. Max tries her best to believe that a miracle might happen.

Chapter Twenty-one

Nan hands me a package. 'I got you a present, love.'

'What for?'

'Just open it, will you?'

I smile and tear the paper. Inside is a genuine, tweed, deerstalker hat, exactly like the one Sherlock Holmes wears.

'Nan! It's magnificent.'

'Do you like it? Put it on!'

I lift it up carefully and try it on.

'Do I look the part?'

'What do you mean: "look the part"? You are the part! You solved a mystery, sweetheart, all by yourself. You've cleared your friend's name. You're an actual, real-life detective now.'

'You don't mind?'

'Mind? Why would I mind? I couldn't be more proud of you.'

'But I thought you didn't really like all the detective stuff. I thought you wanted me to be more, you know ... normal.'

Nan waves her hand in the air. 'Normal? Love, you've got no chance of being normal. Your mum spent half her childhood talking to an invisible gorilla called Tarquin. And look at me – the mad old lady with the hats. Who wants to be normal? I only ever wanted you to be happy, love, and if being a detective makes you happy, that's good enough for me. Now, more importantly, tell me all the gossip. What's the latest on that villain, Josh Ryman?'

'Well,' I say, 'I got the whole inside story from trusted sources.'

'What trusted sources?'

'A bit from Miss Casey, a bit from Tariq and … well, I eavesdropped after Mr Wilson fished him out of the bin.'

'Go on then,' says Nan, leaning in closer.

'Motive – that's always the key. Framing Max wasn't Josh's main motive, that was just an added bonus. His main motive for stealing the money was … well, to steal the money.'

Nan frowns. 'But why would he do that? I thought he was spoilt rotten, had everything he wanted.'

'No, that's what he wanted everyone to think.

His dad never really bought him all the stuff he said he did. Remember I told you he was always going on about his iPhone – how he couldn't bring it to school because it might get confiscated – it was all lies. He never had an iPhone, or an X-box and his dad never gave him £20 a week pocket money. Josh stole the money because Tariq got a phone for his birthday and started texting Josh. Josh was running out of excuses for why he wasn't replying. He had to get a phone somehow.'

'So what was the money doing in Cuddles' cage? He wasn't going to get a phone in there,' Nan asks.

'He got scared. He was waiting for the fuss about the theft to die down before he smuggled the money out of school, but then Max went missing and there were police in school every day. He realised that by planting the key he'd made everyone think Max had run away, and he got really scared about how much trouble he'd caused. He didn't know what to do, so he did nothing. He thought the money was safe where it was.'

'Hadn't banked on you, had he, love?' says Nan.

'He really loved Cuddles, you know. When he found out that Miss Casey made up all the *Spottitummitosis* stuff, he hugged her. She let him go and spend some time with Cuddles in the staffroom while he was waiting for his dad to take him home.'

'Well, maybe being expelled might be good for him: a fresh start. He can go somewhere new and not have to pretend to be Mr Rich Kid.'

'Maybe,' I say.

Nan looks at me. 'I know that face, Lori. I know you're still worried about Max. But you've done a good thing. This is going to help them, isn't it? They'll find her soon, don't you worry.'

I go upstairs to do my homework. I keep the deerstalker on. I reckon it makes a good thinking hat. I'm colouring in arable farming areas on a map of East Anglia when I hear a noise. At first I think it's coming from outside and carry on colouring Norfolk. Then I hear it again: a click and then a crackle. It takes me a few moments to recognise it as the static crackle of my walkie-talkie. Suddenly I remember. Max still has the other walkie-talkie! How could I have forgotten that? What kind of detective am I? I stand up and start frantically running around the room looking for it. I find it in my drawer and quickly press the receiver button.

'Hello! Hello! Max? Is that you?'

'Hello.'

'Max. It's me, Lori! Where are you?'

'Hello?' says a voice again. It doesn't sound like Max.

'Who's that?'

'Where's Martin gone? I was talking to Martin. Who are you?'

'What? This is Lori. Lori Mason.'

'I think we've got our channels crossed. Sorry. I think it's my walkie-talkie, I keep picking up other people's communications. I'm trying to tell my mate Martin about the fish I've just caught. Maybe if you turn your receiver off, I can get back to him.'

My heart sinks. 'Right,' I say. 'Sorry…'

'Hang on,' says the voice. 'What did you say your name was?'

'Lori Mason.'

'I thought that's what you said. Listen, someone keeps looking for you on here. All the bloody time. Keeps coming through on my walkie-talkie. "Lori Mason, can you hear me?"'

'That's Max! What else does she say? Where is she?'

'No idea, love. I've heard it a few times, though, over the last few days and in the evenings, too. She's scanning the frequencies looking for you. You must be out of range. They only cover…'

'Three kilometres. I know. Where are you when you hear her?'

'Here by the river, down in Edge Hill Park. I only ever use the walkie-talkie when I'm fishing. There's no mobile signal here.'

'If you hear her again, ask her where she…' The radio starts to crackle again. 'Hello! Hello! Can you hear me? Are you still there?'

The line's gone dead.

Chapter Twenty-two

Max is working her way through lots of detective books while she is a prisoner. Julie brings her piles from charity shops. Sometimes she skips through the boring bits. There's a bit too much about weather and hats and not nearly enough about exotic animals, but she is learning from them. The main revelation is that nobody says what they really mean in detective books. Everyone tries to trick each other. Every story involves lies, hidden messages and traps.

When Julie arrives in the morning, Max puts on her worried face.

'What's up with you?'

'Nothing.' Max knows this is the one word guaranteed to make an adult more curious.

'Well, there's something. You've got even more of a face on you than usual.'

'It's just, I've been thinking … what happens if the stolen money turns up?'

Julie shrugs. 'So?'

'Well, if I don't have the money, how am I surviving as a runaway?'

'I told you before – you're sleeping rough, stealing food, that kind of thing. We've been through this.'

'But I'm supposed to be running away because I'm in trouble. If I didn't steal the money, there is no trouble to run away from.'

'Why don't you just leave the worrying to me?' She turns back to her phone. She always does that when she runs out of answers.

'It's just…'

'What?'

'Well, I was thinking. I don't think people will really believe I've run away. That just isn't me. I'd always let my mum know I was OK.'

'For the last time, you're not seeing your mum.'

'But why don't I send a letter? I could say clearly then that I've run away. Tell her not to worry. Otherwise, if they find the money, they might start thinking I've been taken and then they'd start searching everywhere – it'd be more risky for you.'

Julie considers this for a second, then shakes

her head. 'Nah, no chance. She'll just have to worry.'

Max waits for a while and then says, 'If only there was some way to make it look as if the note came from somewhere else...'

Julie looks at her. Max pretends to read and waits for the rusty wheels inside Julie's head to turn.

'Wait a minute!' Julie says excitedly. Max lowers her book innocently. 'I've got an idea. Another Julie Plan! You could write your little note and then I could send it from somewhere totally different ... like London. Yes! Get a London postmark on it! They'd start looking for you there. There are thousands of runaway kids in London. That'll keep them busy.' She looks so pleased with herself.

'Wow,' Max says, 'that is really good thinking.'

Chapter Twenty-three

Miss Casey tells me to go to Mr Wilson's office but when I get there Mr Wilson is nowhere to be seen. Instead Detective Superintendent Alison Burrows is sitting in his chair.

'Hello, Lori.'

'Hello.'

'I hear it was you who cracked the case of the stolen charity money.'

'Oh, yeah. Well I just followed the evidence.'

Alison Burrows smiles: 'You're a clever girl. We could do with more like you in the force.'

I'm not here to be flattered. I get straight down to business.

'So, I suppose this changes things, anyway.'

'In what way?'

'Well, now you know Max can't have run away. She didn't take the money, so she didn't need to run away. And obviously she's had no money to buy food and stuff with…'

'We're keeping an open mind and following up all leads.'

'Good, because I've got a very important lead for you.'

'Oh, yes?'

'Last night I got a message on my walkie-talkie from a man. It was a crossed line. He was trying to talk to someone called Martin about a fish, but he got me instead. Then, when he heard my name, he said there was someone scanning the frequencies every night. Someone looking for me!' Alison Burrows carries on looking at me. For some reason this isn't sounding as convincing as I thought it would. I get the uncomfortable feeling that Alison Burrows might think I'm mad. I try again.

'Don't you see? It's Max! She's got my other walkie-talkie. It means she's somewhere within a mile or two of Edge Hill Park.'

'I'm sorry, Edge Hill Park?'

'Yes, that's where the man was fishing. For him to pick up her message, he must be within a three-kilometre range of wherever she is, because that's the maximum range of the Kommunicator 150 system.'

'I see. Did Max identify herself to the man?'

'Well, no, I don't think so. He didn't say anyway. Just that someone was looking for me and obviously that can only be Max, as she's got the walkie-talkie.'

'Do you know for a fact that she has the walkie-talkie with her?'

'She must have if she's using it!'

I'm not sure Alison Burrows is that bright. She's quiet again for a long time, deep in thought. Finally, she says, 'OK, Lori, I'll talk to this man. Follow it up. What's his name?'

'Well…' I bite my lip. 'I don't actually know his name. We lost contact before he could tell me. But he has a friend called Martin and he fishes in Edge Hill Park. I mean, I'm sure you could find him.'

She takes off her glasses and rubs her eyes.

'Lori, what exactly is it that you think has happened to Max?'

'I think…' But now for some reason I find it hard to speak, there's an annoying lump in my throat. 'I think,' I try again, 'that maybe she's been kidnapped.' I take a deep breath. 'There are things you don't know.' I speak in a low voice. 'I promised I'd never tell anyone, but … Max's dad gambles. All the time. He owes lots of money to lots of bad men. Criminals. I think maybe one of them has taken Max to get money from him.'

'A ransom?'

I nod.

Alison Burrows gives me a kind smile. 'Lori, you're a clever girl and I can tell you're interested in detective work, probably read every detective book under the sun, I know I had at your age. But the thing you'll learn when you grow up and become a real detective – as I very much hope you will one day – is that life isn't much like detective books. People don't always act in the way you think they will. Sometimes people do unexpected things. I really appreciate everything you've told me today. First of all, I want to reassure you that we already know all about Max's dad's gambling issues, and we've looked very closely indeed at his associates but, as you know, nobody has demanded a ransom, so it doesn't look as if money is a prime motive here.

'The thing is, Lori, the reason I came today is to tell you that we've received a letter from Max that seems to confirm our belief that she's run away. It doesn't mean we're not looking for her. Of course we'll keep looking for her, but it does look as if she has chosen to go away for herself. The letter was addressed to her mum but she wanted to pass on a message to you, too. Here, you can read for yourself.'

She hands me a photocopy. There's no mistaking Max's long, spidery handwriting.

Dear Mum,

I'm so sorry for the worry I've caused you. I want you to know that I'm OK and I can look after myself. I had to get away, Mum. London is fine, I'm being careful and I have money to get by. I love you and this is not your fault.

Please say sorry to Dad too in case he is worried.

Also to Lori. I miss her and Peggoty but not Dandybird. Tell her to keep up with the detective work.

I'm sorry if I've let everybody down. Please don't worry about me and take care of yourself. Love

Your Maxie

Xxx

I carry on staring at the piece of paper for a long time after I've finished reading it. Eventually, I speak.

'What does she mean "London"?'

'It looks as if that's where she is. The letter was postmarked there.'

'But that's more than three kilometres away. It doesn't make sense.'

'Look, Lori, I'm not sure the walkie-talkie witness really stands up. We don't know who this man is. He might have just been pulling your leg. There are some strange people out there.'

She points to a line in the letter. 'Can you tell us who Peggoty and Dandybird are?'

'Peggoty is a cat. I've never heard of Dandybird.'

'Is it your cat?'

'No. I'm allergic. It's the cat from the sweet shop, Max always makes a fuss of her.'

'I see. Is it possible that Dandybird is another animal?'

I shrug. 'Maybe. Max is nuts about animals.' I'm not really interested. I'm still trying to take in the note.

I walk back to the classroom in a daze. The

first thing I see as I open the door is Max's face staring back at me from everyone's "Find Max" T-shirts. She looks as if she's smirking.

Chapter Twenty-four

Last night Max had the sweet-factory dream again. Only this time it was more like a nightmare. The sweets were passing by too quickly and she was having to try and stuff too many in her mouth. The man with the notepad was getting cross because he couldn't understand anything she was saying. Sweets started flying off the orange conveyor belt and suddenly an alarm started sounding. The factory had to be evacuated. Max ran and ran but still the beeping sound followed her. She woke up and realised that the sound was not in the dream. It was there in her room. She was sitting up trying to make sense of the noise when she realised. It was the call signal! The walkie-talkie! She grabbed it from under her pillow and pressed the receiver button:

'Lori. Lori. It's me! Can you hear me! Over.'

The radio crackled briefly and then died. She tried again and then again. She shouted into it as if that would work and that's when she noticed:

the red power light wasn't on any more. The battery had died.

Max shouted out every bad word she could think of at the very top of her voice but at the end of it she felt just as frustrated as before, but now she had a sore throat to go with the frustration as well. She asked herself what would Sherlock Holmes do? Or Miss Marple? Or Lori? And she realised that the answer was: think.

The next morning, she mentioned to Julie that it was really driving her nuts never knowing what the time was, or how long she should sleep or how many hours till the next meal. She asked, in her nicest possible voice, if there was any chance she could have a small clock in the room. Julie thought for a minute but could see nothing suspicious in a clock. She said OK she'd bring one next time. Max smiled a grateful smile. She thought of the batteries. The Kommunicator 150 would soon be back in action. Detective stories were all just lies and traps.

Now Max hears footsteps coming up the stairs and waits eagerly to see the clock, but instead, for the first time since she arrived, Max hears another voice. A man is speaking quietly, but angrily.

'I'm not coming in there with you. What? Do you think I'm as stupid as you are?'

'Keep your voice down,' Julie says. Max hears a creak and then the thud of a door. Their voices are muffled now. They're in the next room. Max gets up and quickly tips her glass of pop down the sink. The wall is paper-thin and when she puts her glass up against it, she can hear the man's voice clearly.

'You've lost your mind.'

'I thought you'd be pleased. £50,000! I get half and half goes to the dad. Only he owes most of that to you, so we end up with all of it! You were giving out about the money he owes you and I came up with a plan to get it all back … twice over!'

'You ain't gonna get that reward. Can you really be so thick? The first thing the police will do is investigate anyone claiming the reward. You're going to be their prime suspect.'

'No, you don't understand. I won't be a suspect. I'll be a hero.'

'No, Julie, you don't understand. Anyone who makes any money out of this is a suspect.'

'Well, let them suspect. I don't have a criminal

record. I've always been very careful about that. They can investigate and they'll find nothing.'

The man shouts something angry-sounding, Max doesn't think it's even a word.

'You're my girlfriend! You're connected to me! I'm connected to her dad! He owes me money. It will take them five minutes to work that out.'

'Well, I don't see how.'

'You don't see lots of things, Julie, but it don't mean they're not there. I've told you before about interfering.'

Max's mum always said it was wrong to eavesdrop, but Max is sure there are exceptions and that this must be one of them. She can't help grinning as she hears Julie being told off.

'Do I have to spell it out to you?'

He's speaking more quietly now. Max has to really crush her ear up against the glass.

'You're being a pessimist, Karl. I don't know if I've told you before but you can be a real downer at times. You're just jealous because you could never have come up with a plan like this.'

'You're right, I couldn't. I'm nowhere near stupid enough. If you carry on, you're going to go to prison for a very long time. Worse, I'll be in prison, too, because they won't believe for a second that I had nothing to do with this. Nobody in their right mind would ever believe that this was all just some lovely surprise you were hatching for me.'

Julie's quiet.

'You've kidnapped a little girl,' he says.

'Don't say that. That makes it sound bad. It's not a kidnapping, it's a fake kidnapping! There's a big difference, Karl. I've looked after her. Multipacks of crisps and everything. More than her dad ever did.'

'You locked her up, Julie. Wake up. Nobody likes child kidnappers. Not even other criminals. Do you know what prison's going to be like?'

Max wants to go and shake this man by the hand. He's finally talking some sense into Julie.

'So, what are you saying?' says Julie. 'I just let her go? After all this?'

'You didn't even disguise yourself.'

'What's that got to do with anything?'

'She can identify you!'

'So, now you're saying I'm going to go to prison even if I let her go.'

'That's what I'm saying.'

'Well, that doesn't make any sense. Prison if I go ahead, prison if I don't. You're not giving me any options.'

'You haven't given yourself any options ... except one.'

They're silent for a long time. Max tries to imagine what the option could be. She starts to have a very bad feeling.

'No,' says Julie. 'I don't think I like what you're saying.'

'We've got to act and we've got to act soon. Every day she's here is another day the police might find her. I'll be back tomorrow night. You've left us no choice. We've got to get rid of her.'

Chapter Twenty-five

I'm standing in Meacham's sweet shop, though I don't really understand why. It's obvious that Max has run away to London. The evidence couldn't be clearer: a letter in Max's handwriting, postmarked London. And I know that a good detective should always follow the evidence ... But sometimes, very occasionally, even a good detective has to follow a feeling, or if you want to use the correct TV cop terminology: a hunch. Good detectives follow the evidence; brilliant ones follow their hunches. That's what I'm trying to tell myself anyway.

This is the line in the letter that I can't quite get past: '*I miss her and Peggoty but not Dandybird. Tell her to keep up with the detective work.*'

Why would Max mention Peggoty to me in the letter? I don't even like the cat. And who or what is Dandybird? Alison Burrows would say I read too many detective books, but what does she know. It feels like a clue or a coded message. I think Max is trying to tell me something and the only concrete clue I have is a fat, fluffy cat that makes me sneeze.

I pick up a Curly Wurly and take it up to Mr Meacham behind the counter. Nan is excellent at making conversation with shopkeepers. If it was an Olympic sport, she would definitely be a gold medallist. I think it must be a skill you develop as you get older. This situation, though, demands that I make apparently casual conversation with Mr Meacham, so I imagine I'm Nan and go for it.

'Good morning. How is Peggoty?'

'I beg your pardon?'

'Peggoty, your cat. I would like to know how she is. It's a casual enquiry.' This is harder than it looks.

'Oh, well, thank you for your casual enquiry. Peggoty is fine as it happens. Be useful if she caught a mouse once in a while, instead of sitting about all day like the Queen of Sheba, but we can't have everything.'

'I see. May I make another enquiry?'

'You may.'

'You don't happen to have another cat or pet of any kind called Dandybird, do you?'

'Danny Bird?'

'Dandybird.'

'No, afraid not. One pet's enough. Sounds like a good name for a budgie to me.'

'And do you know anyone who has a budgie?' I try.

He rubs his chin. 'My auntie Peggy in Whitstable.' I quickly get out my notebook. 'But both she and the budgie have been dead for over fifteen years.'

I put my notebook away and pick up my Curly Wurly. 'OK, well, thanks for your help, anyway.'

Mr Meacham smiles. 'Thank you for your enquiries.'

As I make my way to the door, I notice an old-fashioned wooden crate of pop on a stand at the side of the shop. Something makes me stop to look and that's when I see it: a line of bottles of Dandelion and Burdock.

Dandybird! Dandelion and Burdock! Max's favourite drink. Could that be what it means? My brain suddenly turns into a massive police computer churning this new information and all its implications. Max misses Peggoty, but she's not missing Dandybird. Why? Does that mean she's still getting Dandelion and Burdock wherever she is? Her mum said that Meacham's was the only place she knew that still sold it. Mr Meacham might hold vital information!

I take a bottle up to the counter. Mr Meacham looks up from his paper:

'Back again? More pet enquiries?'

'Moving on to soft-drink enquiries.'

'Of course.'

'Do you sell much of this?' I say holding up the bottle.

'Well, now, it's funny you should ask that.' He leans forward as if sharing a secret. 'If you'd have asked me that exact question a few weeks ago, I'd have said, "Hardly any." I drink most of it myself. It's what I used to drink as a kid, but of course no one likes it these days. Unfashionable, rather like me.'

'But what would you say if I asked you today?'

'As you just did.'

'As I just did.'

'I'd say that, suddenly, in the last week or two, we've started shifting some. It's always the same customer, a lady who comes in most mornings and buys a bottle of that and a whole load of sweets and crisps.'

I have a tingling feeling all over my body.

'Does she ever buy any kola kubes?'

'You know her, do you? Yes, always 100g of kola kubes, too. I'm surprised she has any teeth left in her head. Not that I'd say that. It's not good business sense for sweet-shop proprietors to mention dental health, plus she's not the chatty sort, to be honest. Bit of a sour look about her. Maybe that's why she needs all the sugar.' We both laugh at this for quite some time.

Chapter Twenty-six

The next morning, I am in position lurking in the comics and magazines at the rear of the shop when Mr Meacham gives the arranged signal, saying loudly to no one in particular: 'It certainly is a beautiful day. I do miss Paris in the spring.'

Mr Meacham came up with this himself, I really wasn't sure about the Paris bit but he got very excited by the idea of giving a secret signal. The only problem is that it's clearly not a beautiful day and the blonde woman who has just entered is confused by the comment.

'What are you talking about? It's drizzling!'

'Beautiful for the flowers, I meant,' says Mr Meacham with a beaming smile.

The woman is somewhere in her thirties and wearing a black, hooded anorak. She goes over to the display stand and I watch covertly as she selects a bottle of Dandelion and Burdock and two packets of smoky bacon crisps. She asks Mr Meacham for 100g of kola kubes and stops for some time to scan the front pages of all the newspapers before paying and leaving. Mr Meacham winks at me as I follow her.

'Is that Danny Bird?' he whispers.

I give him the thumbs up and leave.

My plan is to get the subject's car registration number and take it straight to Alison Burrows. But when I get out of the shop, I see that there is no car and the woman is already halfway down the road, walking quickly, head down, looking at her phone. I look around and then start jogging as discreetly as I can behind her, ducking into doorways and behind parked cars every now and then for no real reason except that's what people do on telly.

Fifteen minutes later, we reach the edge of the Glebe estate. The high-rise tower blocks on the estate are the tallest buildings in New Heath by miles. My dream has always been to live on the top floor of one of them. From up there I'd have an amazing, birds-eye view of any suspicious activity happening down on the mean streets below. I'd set myself up in a nice comfy chair by one of the big windows with my binoculars, or better still a camera with one of those enormous long, zoom lenses. I'd have a bag of Maltesers on my left. Soft drink of choice on my right. It would be total crime-spotting luxury. The only problem is that they're going to demolish all the blocks soon, so that's one dream that's never coming true.

Parka woman doesn't go toward the tower blocks, though. Instead she heads for a row of small, empty-looking houses on a short path some distance away from the nearest road. I watch her go into number eight, the house at the end of the block. I make a mental note of the street name and hide behind a big bush. There's loads of litter trapped on the branches which provides extra cover. Perfect. I begin my surveillance.

Now I'm here, staring at a closed door, I start to wonder again if I'm doing the right thing. I mean, I realise that criminals don't go around with stripy tops, eye masks and big sacks marked 'Swag' on their backs, but parka woman really doesn't look like an evil kidnapper; she looks more like somebody's mum. Maybe she's just an innocent person with a very sweet tooth. Maybe I've got carried away, just like Alison Burrows said.

I start worrying about needing the toilet. This never seems to happen to detectives on a stakeout on telly. What do they do? Do they wee in their cars? I'm wondering how long this all might take, when the door opens again and the woman comes out carrying a black bin bag of rubbish. She leaves the front door open as she struggles up the path with it. If Max is in that house, then the bin bag will be full of real evidence that I can take to Alison Burrows.

The woman goes to the side of the house to open a gate and drag the wheelie bin from the back garden. I look back at the open door, straining to see any evidence of Max inside. I feel calm and in control for the first time since parka woman entered Meacham's. Once she goes back indoors I can grab the bin bag and take it away somewhere safe to investigate. All I have to do is wait. But my eyes keep turning back to the open door. What if Max is inside right now?

My heart starts beating crazily and suddenly, without my brain's permission, my legs are pushing me up from behind the bush and I'm running faster than I've ever run in my life, straight for that door.

Chapter Twenty-seven

I'm hiding in a complete stranger's loo. This was the first door I came to inside the house and I dived in, breathing heavily, my heart beating so loudly I'm sure parka woman will hear it from outside. I am trespassing. I have broken the law. I look down at my legs in horror. They are criminal legs. I hear the woman's footsteps coming back up the path and I hold my breath. Two scenarios instantly pop into my head:

1) the woman is completely innocent. She'll find me, call the police and they'll lock me up.

2) the woman is an evil kidnapper. She'll find me, not call the police and she'll lock me up.

I'm trying very hard to think of a third, less terrifying outcome when I hear the front door slam and footsteps moving away, going back up the path. Parka woman's gone out! She was just putting the rubbish out before leaving the house. I let out a very long breath and wait for the feeling that I'm about to have a heart attack to pass.

When I've calmed down, I start searching the ground floor, though it's pretty clear straight away that this has been a terrible mistake in every possible way. This is not a kidnapper's den. It's a totally normal house: 'Keep Calm & Carry On' mug on the draining board, *OK Magazine* on the sofa. There's no trace of Max anywhere. I sit down on the bottom step of the stairs. How could I have got so carried away? Dandybird? What was I even thinking of? What would Nan think if she could see me now, trespassing in a stranger's house? I put my head in my hands.

I don't hear any footsteps. The first thing I hear is the jangle of keys on the other side of the front door. I stand up so quickly I feel dizzy. I run from the front door, down the hall and just manage to throw myself into the understairs cupboard as I hear the key turn in the lock. There are coats hanging on the back of the cupboard door and it's only then that I realise my mistake. This is parka woman! The first thing she's going to do is take off her parka and hang it in the exact place I'm standing. I push myself as far back in the cupboard as I can and crouch down low behind a vacuum cleaner. I hear her footsteps getting closer and then the creak of the door opening. I hold my breath. I try to will my heart to stop beating. The woman stands a few feet away from me. I can hear her breathing. She doesn't take off her coat. Instead she moves coats around, from hook to hook. I hear her muttering, 'Where is it?' before finally grabbing an umbrella. The door closes and, a moment or two later, I hear the front door slam again.

I need to run as fast as I can, out of this house and far, far away and never look back again, but I know I have to wait just a few more minutes to make sure the woman is out of sight. As I crouch in the dark, I realise that it's time I gave up my detective dreams. Crime isn't a game. Nan's right, I need to live more in the real world. It's time to grow up.

I count to a hundred and finally get out of the understairs cupboard. I head to the porch and sneak a look through the side window. There's no sign of the woman, or indeed anyone, around. I decide then that the first thing I'm going to do when I get out of this house is dump my secret notebook in the wheelie bin. I'll go home and tell Nan I've decided on a career change. Maybe I could be a teacher, I couldn't be too much worse than Miss Casey. I mean I'm good at remembering names and I've been able to clap for as long as I can remember.

I reach up to open the door when I hear a noise. A creak or a squeak from somewhere. I don't care. Probably the neighbours. I just need to get out. I open the front door and remember the house next door looked empty. I stand on the threshold, willing myself to slam the door behind me and leave. But the estate is deserted. If I heard a noise, it can only be coming from this house.

I look over my shoulder and back up the stairs. It could be anything. Could be parka woman's husband. Could be a vicious pet dog. Could be a hundred and one things that will put me in even deeper trouble. But then it could – just very slightly possibly – be Max. I close my eyes and think 'What would Sylvie Clandestino do?' Slowly I close the door and go back inside. I've only done half the job I came to do. I have to check upstairs.

I tiptoe as silently as I can until I reach a landing with four closed doors. I listen at each one but the only thing I can hear is the blood hammering in my ears. I try the first door as gently as I can, moving the handle very slowly, opening the door a tiny crack. It looks safe. I open the door fully and see a neat, empty bedroom. That's when a voice nearby makes me jump out of my skin.

'Julie?'

I dive behind the door to hide.

'Julie? Is that you?'

I recognise that voice. I come out from behind the door and stand in the middle of the landing.

'Max? Max, is that you?'

There's a pause and then I hear her voice clearly coming from the door straight in front of me: 'Lori?'

'Max!' I try the door but it's locked. 'Are you OK?'

'Yeah. I'm OK. You need to find the key.'

I look around desperately and try to think. Where would a criminal mastermind hide a key they didn't want anyone to find? It could be anywhere in the house. It could even be with the criminal mastermind right now. Maybe they keep it in a safety deposit box in a bank. That's when I see a wooden key rack hanging on the wall right ahead of me. It has a motto printed on it:

'Hang it where it's plain to see, then you'll never lose that key.'

I shrug. Maybe not a criminal mastermind, but still sensible advice. I grab the key off the hook and quickly open the door. Max is standing on the other side, grinning: 'Lori Mason Private Detective. What took you so long, partner!'

Chapter Twenty-eight

Oh no. Not again! Max and I are halfway down the stairs when we hear it. The unmistakable sound of the key turning in the front door.

We look at each other for a micro-second and then turn around and run full-speed back upstairs. The front door creaks open as we pile into Max's room and look for somewhere to hide.

'The key! The key!' hisses Max and grabs it from me, running back to hang it up outside on the landing as we hear voices coming up the stairs.

She dives back into the room and closes the bedroom door as silently as she can, bundling us both through into the en-suite. She turns the shower on full blast, presses her ear up against the door and listens. When we hear the rattle of the key on the rack, she calls out loudly, 'Julie?'

'Yeah.'

'Don't come in, please!'

I can picture parka woman, just outside the

door, key in hand, poised to put it in the lock and discover it's already unlocked.

'What do you mean?'

'I'm in the shower. I'm not dressed.'

We hear a man's voice. 'That's brilliant, that is. Just what we need. I just want to get this over with.'

'Shut up, Karl,' she hisses and then in a louder voice calls out, 'Listen, Max, there's a nice man here, a friend of mine, and he really wants to talk to you about something, so are you almost done?'

I shake my head crazily.

'No, I'm definitely not almost done,' says Max quickly. 'Only just this second got in…'

I hold my nose and point at her.

'And … and … the thing is I'm really very grubby. I haven't had a shower since I've been here … so I really need a good, long shower.'

'Eeeuw,' says the woman. 'I'd say you do. Alright. We'll get a cup of tea. Don't be long, though.'

We hear footsteps go downstairs and I breathe out for what feels like the first time in days.

'Give her a minute,' whispers Max.

We leave the shower running and go back

through the bedroom. We open the door a crack to check the coast is clear and then very rapidly close it again. A man sits at the top of the stairs listening to music on his headphones.

I look at Max and state the obvious. 'We're trapped.'

Max nods. 'Any ideas?'

I close my eyes and think and it comes to me. 'Just one,' I say.

Chapter Twenty-nine

It's been a quiet day down at the river. The fish aren't biting at all. Paul has eaten his sandwiches, drunk his tea, read the newspaper twice – all about the local missing girl – and even done the crossword. He doesn't ever really get bored when he's fishing, but today it's a bit cold and miserable. He thinks of his nice warm living room at home. It's Thursday, which means it'll be cottage pie for lunch. He could be home in half an hour, sat with the wife, food on a tray, watching *Homes Under the Hammer* on catch up. He decides to tell Martin he's had enough. He reaches for the Kommunicator 150, but it seems like Martin's beaten him to it as the walkie-talkie crackles into life before he's had a chance to speak.

'Come in, please. Come in, please. Anybody. Can you hear me? Urgent assistance required.'

'That's not you, Martin, is it?' says Paul.

'You can hear me! This is Lori Mason...'

'Oh, hello again...'

'Hello, listen. Please! This is an emergency. Missing girl Max Ellington is being held at number 8 Cattells Drive on the Glebe Estate, I repeat number 8 Cattells Drive. Tell the police come quick. Lori Mason is with her. We're in danger.'

Paul is already on his feet. 'I got it. Number 8 Cattells Drive. Hold tight there, Lori. There's a phone box two minutes away.'

Paul scrambles up the river bank. The cottage pie will have to wait.

Chapter Thirty

Six months later

The charity shops of New Heath are filled with old 'Find Max' T-shirts. Passers-by still sometimes recognise her in the street; she's a local celebrity. The sight of her cheers them up. 'A good news story for once!' they shout; or 'Hope your life's back to normal now, love.' Max smiles shyly and says, 'Yes thanks.' But she's not really telling the truth. Her life is not back to normal. Normal was changing schools every six months, switching off in class and having no friends. Why would she want to go back to that? Since Lori found her, Max can't help but notice that no one's life has gone back to normal.

Julie
… is in prison awaiting trial, along with Karl. Julie still doesn't really understand what actually happened on that last day. Suddenly everything went very

wrong. When she went upstairs to check what was going on, she found the bedroom door unlocked and some random other girl standing next to Max. It was one of the few occasions in her life when words completely failed Julie. She remembers Karl panicked. 'There's two of them! Oh my God, they're multiplying!' And then a loud crash and police officers were everywhere.

Julie Pickering is her full name but the newspapers just call her 'Evil Julie'. Privately, Max thinks 'evil' is a bit much. Julie isn't evil. She's greedy and not very clever, and that's just a really bad combination.

Max thought at first that a prison sentence was a bit tough on Karl as none of it had been his idea. But Lori reminded her that in the end he was the one who wanted to 'get rid' of Max. When she remembers that Max feels less sorry for him.

Lori

… got the £50,000 reward for finding Max. But Lori said she was only able to do it because of Max's coded message in the letter, so she gave half to Max. Despite the money, Lori still hasn't changed her bedroom into the kind of slick detective office she's always dreamed of. She reckons she'll stick with the unicorns and rainbows a little longer. She has, though, bought a top-of-the-range leather executive swivel chair from Paperclips Office Supplies. She likes to spin around in it while thinking her detective thoughts.

Detective Superintendent Alison Burrows
… presented both Lori and Max with medals for courage at a special awards ceremony. She shook their hands and said that with their brains and ingenuity they would make brilliant detectives one day. Max smiled politely and said, 'Thanks, but Lori's already a brilliant detective and I'm actually going to be a zoologist.'

Max's dad
… doesn't live with Max any more. She still sees him but, after her abduction, he realised that it was best for everyone if he moved out until he finally beat his gambling problem. He has a job and he's doing OK. Sometimes, when he visits Max, he cries a bit and says he's sorry, and she holds his hand and tells him it's OK. He got her snake charm back.

Max's mum

… and Max have moved to a new flat that doesn't even slightly smell of fried chicken. She has managed to cut down on her medication and no longer sleeps for most of the day. She's started studying Italian and needlework at night school and volunteers at a charity shop which has turned out to be an endless source of crazy hats for Lori's nan.

Lori's nan

… has realised that she is a born campaigner. After happily disbanding the Find Max Campaign, she has set up a national missing pet website – lassiecomehome.com – with her friend Mad Marjorie and her neighbor, Mrs Cromarty. The logo is a dog dressed as Sherlock Holmes.

Christina Aisley

… visited the Great Wall of China with her family last month. Her brother Kieron told Max that it was definitely the best wall he'd ever travelled halfway across the world to see. Max thinks he'd still have preferred Disneyland. Christina loved the wall so much she even sent a postcard to Josh

Ryman telling him that she forgave him for stealing all her collection money.

Josh Ryman
… goes to a different school now where he's tried to turn over a new leaf. He volunteers at the local animal shelter and has taken up the clarinet. Max sees him sometimes walking round New Heath looking a bit lost. His curls have all been shaved off. He pretends he doesn't know her.

Miss Casey
… finally got a new photocopying card and is always in class on time now. She still calls Max, Maxine.

Mr Cheetham
… is trying to give up smoking. He's quite grumpy a lot of the time, but the bike sheds have never been so clean.

Mr Meacham
… is a little disappointed that sales of Dandelion and Burdock have come to a halt once more. Apart from him, Max was the only person in New Heath

who ever drank it and she never wants to touch a drop in her life again. Peggoty has yet to catch a mouse.

Paul
… caught a lovely big perch last week and got his photo in *Angling News*.

Max
… is the new Hamster Monitor. She's working hard with Cuddles to help him overcome some of his anger issues. He's coming along well.

It's a sort of tradition now that Max and her mum go to Lori's house every Sunday to have a proper roast dinner. Lori's nan will never reveal the secret of her amazingly fluffy Yorkshire pudding, but she has shown Max how to make sensational jam rolypoly. After lunch they normally go out for a walk, but today the rain hammers on the window so Nan suggests that they all stay in and settle down with a pot of tea and a DVD.

'What do you fancy?' she says. 'We've got everything. Well, that's not true. We've got everything to do with detectives and private eyes and that kind of caper; we've got precious little of anything else. Just my Zumba workout DVD.'

Lori and Max's mum are doing the washing-up. Max can hear her mum out in the kitchen trying to teach Lori useful Italian phrases.

'Let's watch a detective one, keep Lori happy,' Max says.

'Have a look through and choose whatever you fancy. Whatever it is, Lori will love it.'

'I've never seen any of *The Clandestinos*,' Max says looking through the pile.

'Who's that, love?' asks Nan.

'*The Clandestinos*.'

'I've never heard of them. What series are they in? I get them all mixed up.'

'No, that's the name of the series. They made loads – back in the Eighties wasn't it? You must have heard of them, they're Lori's favourites. I thought you watched them all the time. All she ever goes on about is Jim and Sylvie Clandestino – her heroes.'

Nan looks at Max with a strange expression.

'What is it?' says Max.

'Jim and Sylvie, did you say?'

'Yeah – Jim and Sylvie Clandestino – the husband and wife crime fighters.'

Nan smiles sadly. 'They were husband and wife alright.'

'What do you mean?'

'Sylvie was the name of my daughter. She married someone called Jim. They weren't on telly and they weren't detectives, they were just Lori's mum and dad. They died back when she was a baby.'

'But…' Max starts to say as her mum and Lori walk back into the room.

'What's up?' says Lori.

'Nothing, sweetheart,' says Nan.

Max smiles at Lori Mason – secret detective, orphan and her best friend. 'I was just saying – shall we have a game of Cluedo?'

The End

Acknowledgements

Thanks to Lucy Luck for agreeing to venture with me into the world of children's literature.

Thanks to Rebecca, Penny and Megan at Firefly for their belief, support and massive lack of nonsense.

Thanks to the Royal Literary Fund for help paying the bills when I was writing this.

Thanks to my family and friends for nothing but encouragement in the face of endless whining and faffing about.

Thanks most of all to Peter, Edie and Dory for seeing it all with me.